IT WAS BOUND TO CRASH

an absurd tale of cops, killers, trains and planes

Saahil Thakkar

This is a work of fiction. The story, all names, characters, businesses, places, events and incidents either are products of the author's imagination or are used fictitiously. Any resemblance to actual events or locales or persons, living, dead or undead, is entirely coincidental.

This story contains some minor expletives and strong language. Any dialogues or characters in this story are not intended to offend the sentiments of any individual, caste, community, ethnicity, culture, traditions, race, or religion or to and support the use or consumption of any type of drugs, alcohol or tobacco products.

No animals were harmed during the making of this story. The publisher does not endorse the views and opinions expressed in this story. The subject matter in this story may be sensitive in nature. Viewer's discretion is advised.

ISBN: 9798844306860
Imprint: Independently published

Cover design by: Saahil Thakkar and Anuraag Soni

This book is dedicated to All The Liars Of The World.
And, The Incompetent Jury of That Screenplay Contest.
Also, Railway Stations.

... I just don't unnerstand it.

MARGE GUNDERSON, FARGO

CONTENTS

Title Page

Copyright

Dedication

Epigraph

CHAPTER 1: SELF FULFILLING PROPHECY 2

CHAPTER 2: SPOONERISM 24

CHAPTER 3: ERISTIC 28

CHAPTER 4: RETROSPECTIVE DETERMINISM 35

CHAPTER 5: HYBRISTOPHILIA 43

CHAPTER 6: ESCHATOLOGY 50

CHAPTER 7: ENFRANCHISED GRIEF 60

CHAPTER 8: VOLENTI NON FIT INJURIA 71

CHAPTER 9: PERJURY 84

CHAPTER 10: STRUCTURALISM 99

CHAPTER 11: THANATOPHOBIA 108

CHAPTER 12: VARDØGER 118

CHAPTER 13: THE MYTH OF SISYPHUS 133

EPILOGUE 143

IT WAS BOUND TO CRASH

Saahil Thakkar

CHAPTER 1: SELF FULFILLING PROPHECY

It was opening night at Jolly Troll, the new posh restaurant on Mountbatten Road. There were celebratory party streamers and balloons put up on the walls to make the opening day seem less lousy than it was. It didn't help much.

Sitting in this restaurant alone were Dheeraj Kumar and his brother-in-law, Sunil Rai, opposite each other. Outside, it had just begun to drizzle, and little raindrops raced down the large window that overlooked the street outside, the window by which the two sat.

Sunil was a bald, fat and powerful looking man. He was wearing a green-collared t-shirt, a brown dhoti and reading glasses as he read the menu, sitting comfortably. Opposite him was Dheeraj, who clearly looked like he didn't belong. Dheeraj had a thin physique. He was wearing a creased white shirt buttoned up to the collar and dark brown pants. His unkempt hair fell over his eyes as he stared at the menu card in front of him, wide-eyed. Behind Dheeraj, a waiter dressed in a tuxedo waited patiently.

After having read enough of the menu card, Dheeraj turned back to look at the waiter behind him, then leaned forward closer to Sunil, lowered his voice to a whisper and asked him, "Bhaiya. Why Have we come to such an-"

Dheeraj turned back again to look at the waiter quietly standing behind the table. Then he turned back to Sunil and continued in an even lower voice, "-such an expensive restaurant?"

Sunil did not whisper back. Instead, in his regular loud booming voice, he replied to Dheeraj, "This restaurant was started by Anuraag, my colleague. I had introduced you during the house-warming, if you remember?"

Dheeraj didn't remember.

"He wanted me to be there on his opening night. Do you need me to cover your bill?"

"No bhaiya, it's fine. I'll manage," Dheeraj replies meekly. He was satisfied with his answer, knowing that he wouldn't manage.

Hoping to change the subject to the reason Dheeraj had called to meet with his brother-in-law that he was slightly afraid of in the first place, Dheeraj started, "Actually, that's what I wanted to talk about. Things at the factory have been a bit-"

Sunil held up his left index finger at Dheeraj mid-sentence and he immediately shut up. Sunil turned to the waiter and motioned him to come to the table. The waiter walked three steps forward and stood directly in front of both Sunil and Dheeraj.

"What would you like sir?" the waiter recited to his first customers of the day.

"What's the deal on these spicy chicken wings?" Sunil asked.

"Sir, if you can finish an entire plate of spicy chicken wings by yourself then you will get a lifetime supply of lemonade, conditions apply."

"What conditions?"

"Sir, only one lemonade per month, lemonade will only be available at this branch, lemonade will only be allowed to the person holding the coupon, lemonade is subject to availability of lemons, lemonade is subject to market risks, lemonade cannot be used to harm or destroy-"

"Alright." Sunil turned to Dheeraj.

"You still have that stomach ulcer acidity thing?" he asked him.

"Actually, bhaiya I-"

Completely ignoring him, Sunil turned back to the waiter before Dheeraj could tell him that yes, he still had a dangerous ulcer in his stomach, and he was not allowed to eat spicy food. "We'll take two plates of the spicy chicken wings and I'll take this Mojito Mint Mocktail, hold the ice."

The waiter scribbled some nonsense into his notepad without looking at it as Sunil spoke and then walked off into the kitchen.

Dheeraj was once again about to start a conversation about the reason he had called to meet him in the first place but before he could start, Sunil was already talking about something else to him.

"You know, 99 times out of 100, what is the reason a new restaurant shuts down?" he asked Dheeraj.

"What? I don't know. Lack of customers?"

"It's rats. It's always rats. Most new restaurants, they have more rats than staff. That's why it's so important for them to select a location properly. Normally, some real estate broker tricks some new owner into buying a property for cheap, then it turns out the whole place is infested with rats. Do you know how many diseases a rat can carry? It was rats that wiped out a third of Europe, you know?"

Dheeraj did not care about the bubonic plague. But he decided to make small talk. "What about cockroaches?"

"Oh no, cockroaches are no problem. They're small, easy to kill and don't really cause much harm. Unless they let a cockroach make it out of the kitchen or let them be found in someone else's plate or something stupid like that, it's really not anyone's concern what they're up to. Cockroaches have their own lives to worry about. It's the rats that pose a real threat to the longevity of the restaurant."

"I didn't know that."

"Well, now you know." Sunil continued. "You know how many rats are in that kitchen over there?" asked Sunil, pointing at the kitchen. Dheeraj thought it was a rhetorical question, but Sunil stared at him with his hand still pointed at the kitchen waiting for him to answer.

"I don't know, bhaiya."

"Take a guess, come on."

"I don't know a lot about rats."

"Come on, just take a guess, alright?"

"I don't know. 5-6?" guessed Dheeraj.

"Thirty-two," declared Sunil, convinced with his extremely specific number. There's thirty-two rats in that kitchen. I can tell. Do you know how they count rats?"

Dheeraj did not know why they were talking about rats. "Don't they just count them one by one?"

"Oh, come on Dheeraj, don't be stupid. You can't just count rats like that, like they're crayons in a box or bullets in a gun or something. They all look the same. Besides, they're always running around. You can't sit them down in a horizontal line and count them one by one. You can't risk miscounting or over-counting. No. What they do is, they check inventory once in the morning when they're opening and once at night when they're closing to measure how much food the rats ate. Then, they divide that quantity by the average amount of food a rat eats, as per information provided by the Health Ministry of India. The number usually depends on the species of the rat so sometimes you must hire outside help to identify the species of rat you have in your kitchen. Anyway, you divide that, and you get the number of rats you have in the kitchen, roughly. If you get a decimal number, always round down. Never round-up. Rats can eat more food than average but never less. Never less."

At this point, Dheeraj was convinced his brother-in-law was bluffing. There was no way this was how they counted rats. "I didn't know that."

Sunil still wasn't done. "For a restaurant of this size, 32 is an appropriate number of rats to have. If this restaurant got a surprise visit from the health inspector and he asked to inspect the kitchen and noticed all 32 of these rats, he wouldn't raise any questions. However, if there were more than 50, well then that would be a problem. You can't have more than 50 rats in a kitchen this size."

"What do they do if there's more?"

"What do you think? They pay off the health inspector. The running rate right now is around five thousand rupees for every additional rat. That's how these restaurants shut down, they have too many rats. By the time the restaurant is able to pay off the health inspector, they're making a loss. Then, they have no reason to continue the business and are forced to shut down."

Before Sunil could go on spewing nonsense about rats, the waiter arrived, with two plates of spicy chicken wings and one mojito mint mocktail. He put down the mint mocktail and one plate of spicy chicken wings in front of Sunil and the other plate of spicy chicken wings in front of Dheeraj.

"Enjoy your meal sir."

"Thanks, you too," said Dheeraj.

The waiter walked back into the kitchen with his tray. Sunil folded his legs up in his brown dhoti on his chair and started eating the chicken wings with both his hands, not caring for how messy he was being. Looking at him, Dheeraj too awkwardly picked up one wing and stared at it. He had been a vegetarian since he was born. He looked up to see Sunil gouging away at his chicken wings and decided he might as well try some himself, rather than starving to death on the restaurant floor, overdramatic as that might be. He took a small bite out of the flesh and within moments, his mouth started to burn, and he started to exhale loudly. The spicy wings were spicy, who knew?

Sunil didn't even react to his brother-in-law and continued to eat his chicken wings, unbothered. Dheeraj however, looked like he was slowly dying right here on opening night of this restaurant. He could barely breathe, and his face was turning into the same shade of red the chicken wings were. Tears were streaming down his eyes uncontrollably, mainly because of how spicy the chicken wings were but also because he regretted every life decision that led him to this moment.

Exhaling loudly out of mouth, tears rolling down his cheek, Dheeraj managed to reach his hand towards Sunil's Mojito Mint Cocktail. As soon as his fingers wrapped themselves around the cold wet glass, they were immediately smacked away by Sunil without him even turning his eyes away from his food.

"If you wanted something to drink, you should have ordered it yourself," said Sunil firmly, his eyes still focused entirely on his spicy chicken wings, not even looking up. Even in his state of extreme pain, Dheeraj was still afraid of Sunil. So, he turned to the kitchen door and loudly wailed out to get the waiter's attention.

"Waiter! Waiter!"

The waiter calmly walked out of the swinging kitchen door and for a moment, Dheeraj could swear he saw a rat on the kitchen floor behind him as the door swung back shut. This was not the time to be worrying about that though.

The waiter walked to his place in front of the table without a single expression behind his face, like he was a robot butler built to serve without the hint of a soul behind his eyes.

"How may I help you sir?"

"Water! Can I have some water? Please?" exclaimed Dheeraj, exasperated.

"Still or sparkling?"

"The regular kind."

"Room temperature?"

"Cold."

"There's no cold water, sir."

"Huh? Why'd you ask then? Just get any water, please! Fast!"

Dheeraj could barely speak, completely out of breath. Yet, with every word he spoke he only exhaled loudly in hopes it would soothe his mouth. It didn't.

"We have *Bisleri*, sir."

"What? No, I want regular water."

"Sir, we only have bisleri water."

"Does that cost money?"

"Yes sir, Rs. 120 for 200ml."

Dheeraj was still exasperated but even in his current state, he didn't know if he was willing to pay this much money for one little bottle of water. He looked down at the red spicy chicken wings on his plate in front of him. He could barely feel his tongue. He didn't have a choice.

"Alright, fine. Just get it fast!"

The waiter was just about to leave when Sunil, for the first time since the plate had arrived, turned his attention away from the chicken and stopped the waiter from going.

"Wait. You're not getting that water," he said.

"Please bhaiya, my mouth is burning!" pleaded Dheeraj.

"Rs. 120 for water, are you crazy? We're not paying this much money because all you eat is bland food and can't handle a little bit of spice, Dheeraj. Grow up."

"Bhaiya please, I need it. I will pay for the bottle myself with my own money."

This offended Sunil. "It's not polite to order food with someone and then order something separately for yourself, even if you pay for it yourself. You're covering the entire bill."

"Alright! Alright! I'll cover the whole bill." The burning sensation in Dheeraj's mouth was somehow getting worse. He turned to the waiter. "Just, please get the water!"

"So that's one sparkling *Bisleri* bottle?"

"Yes! Please! Now!"

"Alright sir, enjoy your meal."

The waiter walked away back into the kitchen and Sunil too, went back to eating his chicken as Dheeraj struggled to breathe. Sunil wiped the red spices off the plate with his index finger and licked it, enjoying every taste. Dheeraj couldn't even get himself to look at the untouched plate of chicken in front of him.

Sunil finished with his plate and looked up at Dheeraj's, as he keenly eyed the kitchen door waiting for the waiter to arrive.

"You mind if I-" Sunil didn't even bother to finish his request as he slowly slid Dheeraj's plate of untouched spicy chicken wings across the table towards himself.

They walked out of the restaurant, Dheeraj following Sunil as he thumped the side of his fist on his chest and burped loudly. Dheeraj had still not gotten around to the reason he had called his brother here in the first place, to talk about money.

"Bhaiya, did you come by taxi?" he asked Sunil.

"Obviously I did. Owning a car in this economy, do I look insane?"

"Actually, I drove the i10 down here. Would you like a ride home?"

Sunil looked around at the road and realised there were not that many autos on the street. Calling a cab would take some time. It was still drizzling but it looked like it might start raining any moment now.

"Alright. Do you mind if I sit in the back?" asked Sunil.

"Statistically the safest part of the car, you know?" Sunil said, as he made himself comfortable in the backseat of Dheeraj's car. Dheeraj adjusted himself in the driver's seat and slowly drove forward. He quietly exhaled. This was the perfect moment.

"Actually bhaiya, I was going to say, I need your help."

Sunil immediately noticed the change in Dheeraj's inflection. "Is that why you called to meet me?"

"Yes, actually."

Before Dheeraj could proceed, Sunil began to guess away. "Is it relationship problems? My sister having those nightmares again?"

"Oh no, Neela is fine. She's sleeping well now. This was actually about-"

"You know how much happier I have been since the divorce?" Sunil interrupted again. "Living by yourself is something, I tell you. You get such control over your life; you really should try it out."

"Bhaiya, I am actually happy with Neela."

"Oh, that's what they all say. 'Happy right now'. You don't know what being happy is until you live alone, you hear me?"

Dheeraj was annoyed that they were going off topic again. "Yes bhaiya, I'll think about that. Bhaiya this was actually about the factory?"

"Business going well?"

"No actually. That's the thing. Recently-"

Sunil interrupted Dheeraj again. "I had told you when you were getting married, remember? Get a salaried job, you'll be happy in life. You know we were going to break off the engagement after we found out you weren't a working man. In our family, we only have salaried working men, that's how you make an honest living. In business, there's nothing but dishonesty, and fraud, and cheating, and treachery. It's all karmic, really. You reap what you sow. You treat someone improperly in this life, you come back as a rat or something. Do you want to be a rat, Dheeraj?"

Dheeraj said nothing. They were talking about rats again.

"I had told Neela, there was still a standing proposal with that guy at my office, Diptesh, nice working brahmin boy, doesn't eat non-veg, very polite, well-mannered and just a very good boy. I told her there was still time for her to change her mind and live an honest, peaceful life. But what does she do? Love marriage. I swear, this entire generation is spoiled with this *DDLJ* concept. 'Love Marriage' it seems, like there isn't any love in other types of marriages."

Dheeraj was nodding along, steering the car yet nervous to steer the conversation back to the point. The windshield wipers swung from left to right in front of Dheeraj. It was raining heavily.

"Some decisions need to be left with your family, they're the only ones that know what's best. Does family ever betray? Family never betrays. Friend, Girlfriend, Boyfriend, all of that has an 'end' at the end. Not Family. There is no end to family. Blood is thicker than water."

Sunil had resorted to talking in *Facebook* quotes now. Dheeraj tried to get to the point again.

"Bhaiya actually, in the factory recently the-"

Sunil interrupted him once again. "Turn here. Take a U-turn, otherwise you will have to go all the way ahead, there's some construction work going on there. God, who knows when all that will end. It feels like it's been going on forever. It feels like Mumbai only, with their metro work going on all the time on every road. You ever travelled by the metro?"

"No."

"So comfortable. So comfortable. They have AC inside, you always have a place to sit, it's perfect. Why do you need to take this car everywhere and cause so much pollution? Just take the metro. Modi is doing so much good for infrastructure in this country. Gujarat model, I tell you."

Dheeraj still nodded along, trying not to lose his patience.

"Ok, stop here. Park here outside only, there's no parking inside," said Sunil. Dheeraj pulled over the car outside a standalone house. "After the divorce, I converted the garage into a pool room. I think divorce is the best thing that can happen to a man, don't you agree?"

Dheeraj didn't say anything. He silently undid his seatbelt and got out. He waited outside for Sunil to get out, but he did not move. For a second, Dheeraj had no idea why Sunil was still sitting inside. Then, he realised. He sighed to himself as he walked over to the backseat door and held it open for Sunil as he exited the vehicle.

"Thanks Dheeraj. God, today's generation has no manners at all. Say, you haven't been over since the *bhoomi poojan* na? Come, I'll show you around."

Sunil started to walk towards his house, but his right leg had suddenly gone limp. Confused with this himself, he took another step, just to confirm. He walked another step towards his house looking down at his leg, but he was only able to limp. It stopped raining.

Sunil turned back suspiciously at Dheeraj, who was just as confused as to why his brother-in-law was suddenly limping. For Sunil, however, his entire aura changed. He seemed much more menacing than usual, more dangerous.

In a suddenly grim voice, he said to Dheeraj just one word. "Come."

Sunil slowly limped towards his door and Dheeraj walked behind him. It was not a very obvious limp, but it was definitely noticeable. Sunil reached towards his door, on which there was no keyhole but instead a password lock. Above the doorbell was a camera, probably to see who was outside. Sunil put the password '121336' and the door unlocked.

Sunil did not say a word. He silently opened the door and stepped inside. A motion sensing light turned on. Inside, there was a screen by the door that showed live footage from outside the door.

Once Dheeraj closed the door behind him, Sunil finally turned back to face him and Dheeraj saw that he had an extremely serious look on his face, making him look scarier than ever.

"Why did you call to meet me, Dheeraj?" he asked, not loudly but very firmly. Dheeraj was confused as to why his brother-in-law's tone had suddenly changed. He didn't know if he should answer. He was finally getting the chance to talk about what he wanted to, but something felt different and foreboding.

Dheeraj decided to answer anyway, although hesitantly. "Actually bhaiya, I've been meaning to tell you. It's kind of a business matter."

"What business matter, Dheeraj?"

There was a strange calmness in his voice, like the eye of a storm.

"It's a business thing, bhaiya. You know, with the recession and everything."

Sunil could tell Dheeraj was beating around the bush. "Don't drag the economy into this. What's the matter?"

Dheeraj was stammering. He could feel his legs shiver and he could barely stand up straight. "Uh. Well, it's- it's for the factory really. For the factory. I was just wondering that, I mean, given the retirement and- your retirement, right? So, I was just thinking that since that I mean you know now that you've got all that- I mean, an investment opportunity, see? It's an investment, really and Neela was telling me about the- the- the invest- how you were looking to invest and everything and I was wondering if you were looking to invest your money and all that. In my factory, I mean."

Dheeraj could barely get through with what he was saying. It felt like his tongue was bigger than his mouth and there were not enough words in the language to translate his idea into words. He kept losing track of each sentence he said and couldn't even think straight. He wondered if he had said anything meaningful at all. Sunil stared at Dheeraj with piercing eyes as he spoke. When he was done, Sunil got one good look at Dheeraj and then turned around and motioned him to follow behind. As they moved, Sunil spoke, "Have you ever seen me limp before?"

Dheeraj was confused. "No bhaiya, did something happen?"

"You tell me."

Dheeraj slowly walked behind his brother-in-law as he limped down the hallway.

"The first time I had this limp, it was in second grade. We were playing football and just my right leg began to hurt like crazy out of nowhere. So, I went to the side and sat down and not even a few seconds after I did, the teacher came and scolded all the boys playing football for bunking class. All the boys except me, because I was quietly sitting in the corner."

The hallway Dheeraj was walking through had paintings on each side of aeroplanes. It looked like a new, recently acquired hobby.

"The next time, it was in sixth grade. I was on the bus, on my way back home from school when my right leg started to hurt again. I limped my way home and lied down on the bed, the next day, I had food poisoning."

Sunil walked into the room on the far end of the hallway and sat down on the chair in front of his desk. He motioned Dheeraj to come inside.

"Then after that, in tenth grade, before my pre-board exam, my right leg hurt again. I ended up failing that exam."

As Dheeraj walked towards the room, out of the corner of his eye he noticed a large hammer kept outside the bathroom. It looked like some construction work had been going on there.

"The last time my right leg hurt like this, Sunandana left me. Do you see a pattern, Dheeraj?"

Dheeraj was standing by the door, listening with his hands turned back and a slightly guilty look on his face. He didn't know why he felt as immensely guilty as he did, but he felt like Sunil was onto him for something he had done.

"Every single time I have a limp in my right leg, something bad happens. I am not one to get superstitious over little things but it's a pattern. I like to think it's God trying to warn me before something bad happens. Before a breakup or before a missed promotion or before my sister marries the wrong guy, my right leg goes limp."

Dheeraj had a worried look on his face, like he was just about to break down and burst into tears. He got defensive and tried to speak up but all that came out was a high raspy voice. He couldn't get words to form again.

"Bhaiya... I just wanted a small loan..."

Sunil's quiet voice, on the other hand, boomed. "I am asking again, Dheeraj. Is everything alright at the factory?"

Dheeraj turned his head down. He subconsciously was backing away from Sunil. Sunil noticed this and stood up from the chair.

This time, his voice was louder. "Have you gotten into some sort of trouble, Dheeraj?"

Dheeraj took a weak pronounced step backwards. Sunil stood looking at his brother-in-law and then took a limped step forward towards him.

His voice got louder. "How much debt are you in, currently? Is it more than you can afford?"

Dheeraj took another step backwards. He turned his head away and saw the hammer lying outside the bathroom.

Sunil's voice got louder still. "Are you drowning in debt and expecting me to bail you out, Dheeraj? Or are you trying to drown me in your debt too?"

Dheeraj looked up to glance at Sunil and realised he was now briskly limping towards him. He looked back at the hammer lying on the floor.

Sunil bellowed, "Answer me, boy!" and in a panicked motion, Dheeraj picked up the hammer off the floor and in an instant swing, he hit Sunil right on his head with it.

As soon as the hammer hit Sunil's head, he just stopped. It was like a switch turned off in his head. He slowly moved his head to look at Dheeraj with a changed expression, one of confusion and slight betrayal, but most importantly, of complete surprise. He raised his left hand to his head where he was struck on his head, at his wound. Then, he brought his palm, in front of his face to see it covered in blood. A stream of thick blood was running down Sunil's head down his cheek, his neck.

If Dheeraj was dumbstruck earlier, now he was almost mute. Fighting through his vocal cords, he started to speak in a whisper, "Bhaiya..." but before he could find words to say, Sunil showed him his left index finger, covered in blood, telling him without any words to shut up. There was nothing Dheeraj could say to defend himself.

Sunil turned his back to Dheeraj and started to limp towards his chair at his desk, very slowly. Dheeraj just stood there at the doorway, watching as his brother-in-law limped towards his desk, his left hand at his head wound again. The head wound he caused. As Sunil moved, he left a trail of blots of thick blood. Sunil pulled a chair and sat down, very slowly, facing away from Dheeraj, looking at his desk.

Dheeraj watched from the doorway as Sunil opened a drawer with his bloody hand, bleeding out of his head heavier still. From inside, he took out one family picture. It was a picture of him, his ex-wife Sunandana, his sister Neela and Dheeraj. Sunil held the picture to the light at his desk, his blood covered thumb covering Dheeraj's face. Then, he slowly placed the picture down at the table.

In a hoarse but firm voice, Sunil let out his final words. "You're a loser, Dheeraj."

Dheeraj didn't react. He watched as Sunil looked at the picture on the table. He just stood there silently in the doorway looking at his brother-in-law lying still on his seat.

Finally, Dheeraj thought to check.

"Bhaiya?" he called out quietly.

There was no response.

"Bhaiya?" he said, a little louder.

Still no response.

For a few seconds, Dheeraj continued to stand there, in the doorway. Then, he looked down and saw the hammer covered in blood.

Dheeraj had no idea what to do. He looked around, trying to understand what the best course of action would be. For some strange reason, Dheeraj wished his wife was here to help him. She always knew what to do. Even if it was her own brother that he had killed.

He slowly walked over to the desk. He was still scared to go close to Sunil, even when he was lying there lifeless. He walked up as close as he could, still wary. He had no idea what to expect. Even after death, Sunil still had a hold over Dheeraj.

Dheeraj had the sudden urge to touch Sunil. He put his hand on Sunil's shoulder and immediately moved it away. It felt strange. There was no longer any Sunil, just a body. Sunil was nothing more than a skin bag filled with muscles and bones. Dheeraj got up close to Sunil's face, looked him right in the eye. Except, there was nothing behind those eyes anymore, nothing looking back. A few minutes ago, there was. Not anymore.

Dheeraj was suddenly aware that he was standing at a crime scene. Soon, there would be police officers right here. He hurried out of the room, through the hallway, towards the kitchen. As he ran, he stepped on a drop of blood on the floor, leaving behind a small footprint of his heel.

In the kitchen, he fumbled around looking for a cloth. Anything to help him wipe the bloodstains. He had never been here before and Sunil had always been a meticulously organised person. There was a drawer here somewhere with five napkins neatly folded and stacked up on top of each other, each for a different kind of stain. With each drawer that he opened and closed to check, he only left more fingerprints around the house, more evidence for the police to find.

In the utility balcony outside the kitchen, Dheeraj found a mop. However, this wasn't the kind of mop Dheeraj was used to. It looked mechanical, an elaborate mop that had a specific spin-action that soaked up water. Dheeraj did not know how to operate it. He picked the bucket that came with the mop up to the sink and switched on the tap, filling it up with water.

On the tap was a water flow restrictor, which meant the bucket filled up very slowly. So slowly that when Dheeraj stood there in the kitchen watching the bucket fill up while there was a dead body of his brother-in-law in the next room, he got restless. Unable to wait there doing nothing, Dheeraj ran back to Sunil's room.

Dheeraj looked around at the scene of the accident. There was a blood covered hammer on the floor, drops of blood on the floor as Sunil walked over to his desk and a lot of blood near the desk all around, including the drawer handle, around the desk, and on the floor under the desk. Dheeraj decided it was up to him to clean all of that up. He wouldn't leave behind a single drop of blood anywhere, bury the body in the backyard and by tomorrow morning, there would be nothing in this house that could incriminate him in any way.

Dheeraj walked over to Sunil again. Something about the lifelessness in his eyes fascinated him. Not just in the philosophical way of trying to understand life after death but also to understand the consequences of his own actions. He had killed him, all by himself. While moments ago, this conclusion scared him, now, in a way it empowered him. His actions had consequences.

Dheeraj stared into Sunil's eyes again and realised he had made a difference to the world. Dheeraj wasn't proud of what he had done but he knew he had done something. How many people can say that they have impacted someone's life in some way? Now Dheeraj could.

In the kitchen, the bucket began to overflow and the sound of water spilling over was loud enough for Dheeraj to run back towards it. As he was running, he stepped on another bit of blood, leaving behind a footprint of his toe.

Dheeraj switched off the tap as the bucket overflowed and he struggled to lift the bucket out of the sink. It was a very big heavy bucket and as he lifted it up, he spilt about a quarter of the water on himself.

He somehow managed to put the bucket down on the floor, creating a mess of spilt water he did. He dragged the bucket to the room and when he arrived there, he ran back to the kitchen to get a mop and returned with it in his hand.

Before anything else, he picked up the hammer with two fingers and put it directly in the bucket. That was one problem he had dealt with.

Then, as he was trying to rinse the mop in the bucket unsuccessfully, the doorbell rang.

Dheeraj stopped dead in his tracks at the sound of the doorbell. He had not expected company. He quietly put the mop down on the floor and carefully approached the door, tip toeing to not make a sound. The doorbell rang again.

The doorway was dark. In the video screen by the door, there was an older woman standing outside. She looked confused as to why the door wasn't opening with Sunil on the other side. Dheeraj tiptoed a little closer to the door very slowly when the motion sensing light detected him and switched on. The older woman on the other side of the door noticed the light switching on from under the door and when the door still didn't swing open like she expected it to, she looked even more confused.

As Dheeraj watched her, hoping she would just walk away, the woman pulled out her phone and started to call someone. Now Dheeraj was confused. Who was she calling?

Then, as if in answer to his query, on the other side of the house in Sunil's room, a phone rang. Sunil's phone.

Dheeraj immediately rushed back through the hallway on his toes towards Sunil's dead body. He noticed the phone ringing in Sunil's front pocket. He walked over a little bit of blood again, this time leaving another footprint of his heel, as he reached inside Sunil's pocket to fish out the phone.

Dheeraj pulled out the phone and placed it on the desk. The contact card read, "Mrs Menka, Neighbour (Old Lady)' There was a green button to accept the call on the left and a red button to end the call on the right as the phone rang. Dheeraj looked at the phone vibrating as the default ringtone played. He turned back nervously towards the front door, now more restless. He was basically jumping in his place looking at the phone waiting for it to stop ringing. Every second felt like forever.

Finally, it stopped ringing. Dheeraj quietly exhaled.

Then, the phone started ringing again and the sudden unexpected sound got Dheeraj by surprise as he nearly screamed, covering his mouth with one hand.

Dheeraj picked up the phone in his hand and after a little deliberation, decided to cut the call. So, he held the red 'end call' button and swiped from right to left. Except, Sunil's phone was different from what Dheeraj was used to because in this one, you had to press the button to end the call. So, he accidentally ended up accepting the call instead.

On the phone, Mrs. Menka spoke, "Hello, Mr. Sunil. This is Mrs. Menka here, head of neighbourhood safety."

Dheeraj clenched his teeth together to mute a loud scream. However, a little sound still managed to escape his larynx and Mrs. Menka heard it over the phone.

"Hello?" she said on the phone, and Dheeraj heard a faint echo from outside the front door. "I can't hear you Mr. Sunil, I think there's a little bit of a disturbance in your network due to the rain. Mr. Sunil, I heard a little commotion coming from your house, so I thought to swing by and check. As the head of neighbourhood safety, it's my responsibility you know?"

Dheeraj was now so visibly agitated now that he just didn't know what to do.

Mrs. Menka continued. "Hello? I can't hear you, Mr. Sunil. Your lights at home are all on sir, even the motion sensing entrance light just switched on. Do you have a cat in there? Because there are no pets allowed on this community, I hope you know. We would have to take strict action if there is a cat Mr. Sunil, like we did with Mrs. D'Souza and her hamster."

Dheeraj was biting his knuckle hard in anger, leaving the mark of his teeth. He just wanted her to go away so he could focus and clean up this whole mess and forget this ever happened and yet, he could think of no way to get her to leave.

"Mr. Sunil, are you there? I cannot hear you, Mr. Sunil. I just called to let you know that as head of neighbourhood safety, it is my responsibility to make sure our community is safe and so I have taken the liberty to enter your premises, just to make sure everything is alright. I hope you don't mind Mr. Sunil."

Dheeraj started to panic. He ran back to the main door, not bothering to tiptoe anymore, to see Mrs. Menka entering the keycode very slowly like how old people often do, referring to a small phonebook in her hand. She had her phone balanced between her shoulder and her ear. Dheeraj was scared for his life. His entire plan was ruined, and the crime scene was now worse than before. He ran back to Sunil's room, looking around for a place to hide. He realised that if he managed to jump out of the window and run through the lawn, he could get out without anyone noticing him. On the phone, Mrs. Menka rambled on.

"... and of course, if there is a cat inside, I will be taking it temporarily until our next homeowners association meeting where we will decide what to do with the cat, the same way we did Mrs. D'Souza's. Don't worry about the cat though Mr. Sunil because..."

Dheeraj heard the door click open and instantly ran to the window and jumped out to escape, and ran straight all the way home, just as Mrs. Menka entered, continuing to talk into her phone. "…I have this cousin that is really good with cats, she will take good care of her."

Mrs. Menka appeared in the hallway, looking around down supposedly for a cat, not noticing the mess of blood or Sunil's dead body yet.

"Kitty kitty kitty kitty kitty kitty?" she called out sweetly.

Mrs. Menka then noticed the blood on the floor. She dropped the phone from between her shoulder and ear, into the mop bucket. In front of her, Sunil lay dead bleeding from his head on his seat, over a puddle of his own blood.

CHAPTER 2: SPOONERISM

Neela was watching television. A particularly gruesome scene from *American Psycho* was on, and Neela was lying down on the sofa wearing a white sweater watching, unbothered by all the gore and screaming. Her eyes on the screen, and she was filing away at her nails without looking down at them.

She heard fidgeting outside the door and put her nail file down and instinctively changed the channel without any reaction. She stood up and went to the door.

Outside, Dheeraj fumbled with the lock to his apartment. His shirt was still wet from when he spilled water all over himself earlier and he was slightly shivering from the cold. Before he could get the door to unlock himself, his wife Neela swung it open.

"Why didn't you ring the bell?" she asked.

"I thought you were asleep," said Dheeraj, taking off his shoes at the door. One look at his wife and he forgot what he had done to her brother. She had a calming presence on him.

"I haven't even had dinner."

"Really? It's past 10, you didn't have to wait up for me!"

"I wasn't. The TV was on and I lost track of time."

"What were you watching?"

Neela looked over at the TV. A documentary about aeroplanes was on.

"Aeroplanes," she replied. "How did your meeting with the investors go?"

Dheeraj stepped into the house and Neela closed the door behind him.

"Too early to tell," Dheeraj replied, walking towards the kitchen.

"Who are they, really? The investors, I mean," asked Neela.

"I told you, just some banker types, looking for good running businesses to take over. You know how it is."

"Is it really like a company or a partnership or just some guy with a lot of black money looking to launder?" asked Neela.

Dheeraj took out a small vessel with chole in it from the fridge and put it on the gas and switched the gas on. Neela sat down on the platform near the gas watching him heat the food.

Dheeraj added a little bit of water to the chole, enough to heat it well. "You need to stop watching so much *Breaking Bad*."

"Do you think selling the factory is a good idea?"

Dheeraj opened a steel box with rotis kept inside. He put one on the open flame on the gas to heat it for a few seconds.

"Profits are on the downswing, now's the best time to sell. Leave before the sink ships."

Neela laughed and at first, Dheeraj didn't realise why. "Ship sinks," Dheeraj corrected himself.

"But what's your plan after you sell the factory? What would you ideally want to do?"

Dheeraj thought about it. With a pair of tongs, Dheeraj flipped the roti on the gas. He reached into a shelf and took out a plate. Then, with the same pair of tongs, he took the roti off the flame and put it on the plate before it started to burn, putting another roti on the gas in its place.

For a few seconds, Dheeraj stared at his wife and forgot he had just killed her brother. "Ideally? Win a lottery and grow old with you in a little house at a hill station farming or raising poultry."

Neela smiled.

Dheeraj used a little spoon to spread ghee evenly over the roti, front and back, then folded it.

"Do you think you're in a position to start from scratch?" Neela asked him.

This was a loaded question. Dheeraj hadn't really thought about his life after selling the factory yet. First there was a headache of looking for someone to sell the factory to. Then the fact that he had just killed his brother-in-law. Dheeraj hadn't had a chance to think ahead into the future. He took the second roti off the gas and started to spread ghee over it.

"I don't know actually," replied Dheeraj. Then, he said something he didn't think he would have said before. "I was thinking I could get a job."

Neela laughed, but sweetly not mockingly. "You'd be terrible at a 'job'. It's just not *you*."

There was a moment of comfortable silence between the two as Neela watched Dheeraj heat up a third roti for her.

Dheeraj hesitantly broke the silence. "Is your brother the type of person?"

Immediately, Neela noticed a change in tone. "That's out of the blue. Why do you ask?"

"I don't know, I was just thinking about him," Dheeraj said defensively.

"Why would you be thinking about him?" questioned Neela.

"I don't know. How can we know why we think something?"

"Is this about asking him for money? This better not be about asking him for money."

"No, of course not."

"Then why bring him up?"

"I don't know, I'm sorry."

"A debt from him is going to bear heavy on us Dheeraj, you know that right?"

"Yes, of course I do."

Dheeraj switched off the gas for the chole. He took a spoon and put the chole on her plate opposite the roti and handed the plate to her.

"Don't ask my brother for money, Dheeraj. That's only going to end badly."

"I know," Dheeraj answered, knowingly.

CHAPTER 3: ERISTIC

In a shadier part of the city that same night, five small time gangsters sat around in a little room. Two sat on chairs, the rest on the bed, watching the television. A shuffled deck of cards lay scattered around the bed, but no one was playing. *Hum Aapke Hain Kaun* played on the TV and some watched, while others looked at their phones. There was no source of light other than the TV in the room with the curtains drawn and tube light off.

Vishwesh and Kaushik, two gangsters, were loudly arguing about the relevance of Chetan Bhagat as an author. The others, used to their constant banter, ignored them as they passionately debated their stance on his place in the history of Indian literature.

"Oh, come on. There's no way you really believe that!" Kaushik said.

"I do, and I'm tired of people telling me otherwise. Chetan Bhagat is not a good author!" retorted Vishwesh.

"What, do you think he just got lucky? Is that how he became the most popular Indian author of all time?"

"First of all, the most popular Indian author is Rabindranath Tagore. Then, it's RK Narayan. Then it's Salim-Javed, and don't try to tell me screenwriting doesn't count. Secondly, just because Chetan Bhagat is mediocrely popular does not mean he's any good at what he does."

A doorbell rang outside and one of the gangsters stood up and went outside the room to the main door, closing the door behind him.

"It's not that he's just popular," said Kaushik. "It's that so many of his books have been turned into movies. How many Indian authors can you name except Chetan Bhagat that got their books turned into movies?"

Immediately, Vishwesh answered, "*Haider*. *Maqbool*."

"They're written by Shakespeare, they don't count."

"*Sacred Games*."

"That's a web series not a movie."

"*Lootera*?"

"The author isn't Indian."

"So not *Saawariya* either then?"

"Nope."

"*Aisha*?"

"Written by Jane Austen."

While Kaushik and Vishwesh displayed their bizarre knowledge of film and literature, one of the other gangsters heard some sort of a quiet commotion outside and went out to go check. He closed the door behind him.

"*Mowgli*?" asked Vishwesh.

"*Jungle Book* was written in India, but Rudyard Kipling was still British."

"He was born in India, he counts."

"He defended General Dyer for Jallianwala Bagh, he doesn't count."

"Yikes. Hussain Zaidi?"

"He writes non-fiction."

"*Devdas*?"

"Too old."

"Oh, come on, that's nonsense!" protested Vishwesh.

"Alright fine, so one," accepted Kaushik.

"Same author wrote *Parineeta*."

"Two then. Chetan Bhagat has written *Hello*, *3 Idiots*, *2 States*, *Kai Po Che*, and *Half Girlfriend*. That's five movies."

Vishwesh brought up a new point. "Just because his books get turned into movies doesn't mean he's a good author."

Before Kaushik can argue, Vishwesh explains himself. "*Hello* was rightfully a flop, *3 Idiots* was good only because Rajkumar Hirani is a master of the craft, *2 States* and *Kai Po Che* were carried by the cast and the soundtrack, and *Half Girlfriend* was terrible."

Kaushik was silent for a moment. Then, as a final attempt of sorts, he asked, "How many of his books have you read?"

"None. How many have you read?"

"None."

They looked at each other awkwardly. Vishwesh stood up.

"I'm going to piss," he announced.

"Nobody asked," retorted Kaushik, as Vishwesh walked over to the washroom just as another crash came from outside the room. Vishwesh gave a confused look towards the closed door and then shrugged and entered the washroom, closing the door behind him, as one should while using the washroom to urinate.

After pissing, Vishwesh reached for the doorknob when he caught a glimpse of himself in the mirror by the door. He washed his hands and put a little water in his hair to fix his hairstyle. Outside, there was the faint sound of people getting beaten up and killed that Vishwesh was too self-obsessed to pay attention to. After perfecting his hair, when Vishwesh stepped out, at first, he didn't notice the bodies.

Then, as his eyes adjusted to the darkness, he noticed that all the gangsters were dead, cut up and bleeding out. *Hum Aapke Hain Kaun* was still playing on TV and in the light from the TV, Vishwesh saw blood spraying out of Kaushik's neck as he motionlessly lay on the chair he was sitting on.

Then, Vishwesh noticed Vetal, out-of-breath. He had a thin face, the kind where you can make out the shape of the skull from under the skin. He had short brown hair cut unevenly, as if he cut it himself. He was wearing a black business shirt and formal black pants and not matching those, brown hunting leather boots. He was holding a big, bloody axe in his hand. His business shirt was covered in blood.

Before Vishwesh could react, Vetal slowly stood up straight and raised his axe as he walked towards him. Under his breath, he was reciting Chapter 2 Verse 27 of the Bhagavad Gita, right as he slashed Vishwesh's neck.

Minutes later, Vetal was doing the buttons to a new, black shirt. He adjusted the collar in the washroom mirror. Vetal noticed a spot of blood on his face by his chin and wiped it away with his thumb, which he washed under running water from the tap.

Then, Vetal switched off the tap and made his way out of the washroom, past all the dead bodies of the gangsters stacked up on the side next to his bloody clothes. He picked up an almost empty suitcase on the floor by the door with one hand and walked out of the door, closing it behind him.

The next morning, Inspector Meera Deshmukh swung the door open and stepped into the crime scene. She was in her late 40s and very clearly looked it. She had been doing this for a long time now. Inside the room, two people from forensics were looking around, marking things. It didn't look like they had found much.

They seldom did.

Meera turned to Sub-Inspector Indravadan, who was already at the scene waiting for her. "Anything? Anything at all?" she asked him.

"An axe," Indravadan told her. "Someone killed these people with an axe, *Parshuram* style, then stacked them up and left."

"Any match on the clothes?" she asked.

"There's a lot of blood. It looks like it's the victims' but with this much of it, it's tough to be sure."

"All of them killed here?" Meera asked.

"No ma'am. Two out in the hall. I think our guy came in from the main entrance, no sign of forced entry so he probably rang the bell, then killed two slowly and quietly, I'm guessing one after another. After that he came in here and killed the other three, stacked them up on the side, God knows why, and changed his clothes and left."

"And the neighbours saw him?" confirmed Meera and Indravadan nodded.

"Yep, they called the police."

Meera bent down to look at the stack of bodies by the door. Indravadan was extremely uncomfortable even looking at the bodies, but Meera was calmly nose-to-nose with the corpses without batting an eye.

"It's Vetal," Meera announced, looking at the bodies. "He's struck again. Call up the station and ask them to send over a sketch of Vetal and show it to the neighbours to confirm his identity."

"He's done this before?" Indravadan asked.

Meera nodded, still looking at the bodies, in deep thought over something. "He's killed three before this. At least we think it's that many, God knows how many he has killed and got away with before that. There's been gangsters turning up dead with similar M.O.s for at least five years, maybe more, but there's nothing concrete connecting the cases together." Pointing to the bodies, she asked, "All of them have a criminal record?"

"Three associated with small-time gang violence, nothing major."

"Why do you think he stacked them up like that?" Indravadan asked.

Meera stood up from the bodies. "It's an ancient wartime thing. They used to believe you carried the souls of all those you killed to heaven one by one. So, tradition was, after a war, all the survivors would lift up the bodies of everyone they killed one by one to the funeral pyres to make sure they were strong enough to do it," Meera explained. "How strong would a man have to be to be able to lift each of them like that?"

"Pretty strong. You need a lot of time in the gym to be able to pull stuff like this."

"Get an idea of his build from the neighbours after they identify him for us. We have to get him."

Meera started looking around the room at the cards on the bed and the TV, now switched off. "Remember that big drug deal gone wrong around last month? Local headlines, three injured, one dead?"

Indravadan nodded.

"All him. He showed up during the deal, chanted a shlok from the Gita and started attacking them with an axe, chanting the whole time. One killed on the spot, another in a coma and third immobilised and unable to speak. All that done by one man. The one in the coma died last week. The third one, he was our sole witness. We barely managed to get a sketch out of him. Then, the next night, Vetal broke into the hospital and killed him. Right under our noses. No one saw him enter, no one saw him leave. He's a ghost. That's why, Vetal."

"Huh?" asked Indravadan, confused.

"Vetal, like the ghost."

"Which ghost?"

"Vetal. Vetal the ghost. From *Vikram-Vetal*."

"Sorry ma'am, I don't watch movies."

Meera looked at him, confused. She checked her watch and then looked at the stack of bodies again.

"Looks like there isn't much else for me to do here. Hold down the fort, let me know if forensics find anything. I'm going back to the station."

"Yes ma'am," said Indravadan.

Meera checked her watch again as she walked out of the front door. She had a difficult conversation with the police commissioner ahead.

CHAPTER 4: RETROSPECTIVE DETERMINISM

Police Commissioner Abhishek Chaubey took off his glasses and wiped them with his shirt on seeing Meera enter. He was an older man that had recently put on some weight he was not very proud of. He had a bushy white moustache and thinning white hair.

"We don't know it's him, Meera."

"Yes we do sir. This matches his M.O. perfectly. He stacked the bodies again, it's definitely Vetal," said Meera, defensively. Every conversation she had with the Commissioner had been an argument every day since he got promoted to the post, but he was one of the few people in the police station that she respected.

The Commissioner put his glasses back on. "That's not proof, Meera. Anyone can do that. Just because I went to the bathroom when India hit a six in yesterday's match doesn't mean my piss had anything to do with Shikhar Dhawan's batting ability."

"Sir, I know it's him. It fits a pattern. He's still in town somewhere. I don't know where but I know he's here. I know it."

"Oh so just because you 'know' it, it becomes proof? I've said it before and I'm saying it again Meera, it's done. Inspector Ajay

Rathode's train will be here this evening please just let him handle this case, alright? You tried your hand at the case, you got nothing, and it's over. Nothing wrong in giving up every now and then, right?"

Meera raised her voice. "Sir, this is my case. I don't want some kid from Mumbai taking over this case he knows nothing about, it's not fair. I've been tracking this guy since the first murder here, I have a right to go after him!"

"A right? *A right?* I allowed you to play around for so long and we have nothing! Let Ajay handle this, alright? We've got other cases to solve. Just last night some woman found this guy murdered in his house, some sort of blunt force trauma on the head. Go check that out, see what you find. Leave Vetal alone, I'm sure Inspector Ajay is capable enough to handle the guy."

"Sir, he's a kid! He's barely out of school and you're handing him our biggest case on his first day?"

"From where I see it, I don't have a lot of options, Meera. You've got nothing, maybe this case could do good with a new pair of eyes on it. Face it Meera, we're getting old."

Meera's phone vibrated in her pocket but she ignored it.

"I'm not getting old sir, and we've not got nothing. Vetal's killed five people today and it doesn't look like he's done. If we don't stop him soon, we're only going to be letting him kill more people."

The Commissioner got annoyed. He didn't like being emotionally manipulated like this. "We don't even know if this was the real Vetal! For all we know it could have just been some *Gangs Of Wasseypur* nonsense! Leave him alone for God's sake!"

Meera was about to scream back when the Commissioner's phone rang on his desk. He raised his index finger at her and she paused in her place.

Indravadan was on the phone. He was calling to let him know

that the neighbours had identified the police sketch. It was Vetal.

The Commissioner hung up the phone and sighed. He looked at the framed picture of Mithun on his desk, next to the picture of his granddaughter. Then, he looked back at Meera.

"Look into this guy that was murdered in his house, I'm assigning you this case. I also expect you to pick up Inspector Ajay from the railway station and make him feel welcome," said the Commissioner. "Allow him to settle into the city for a while, get used to the way things are around here. After that, I'm handing Vetal to him."

Meera smiled at the inspector. "Thank you sir! I'll get him, I promise."

"I don't care. Get out."

When Meera reached Sunil's house, there were already two forensic scientists inside, with Sub-Inspector Gokul ready at the door to brief her. He greeted her and led her inside.

"The neighbour woman discovered the body. She heard some sort of commotion coming from the house, so she called up the owner, Sunil Rai. He's the one that died."

Gokul led Meera inside the house through the hallway towards Sunil's room.

"She says he answered the call but didn't say anything. She rang the doorbell but no one answered, so she let herself in with the password lock. She kept going on and on about some cat but we didn't find one."

Gokul led Meera through the front door and she noticed the video-screen. "Does the camera outside record?"

"No, ma'am." Gokul showed Meera through the hallway and she followed behind him. There was yellow tape around the mop and the bucket and all the drops of blood leading to the desk were marked with yellow post-it notes. He led her into Sunil's room.

"She found the body right there, already dead when she arrived."

Sunil's body was still there on the chair, already showing signs of decay.

"Blunt force trauma to the head, no sign of forced entry, one unidentified i10 outside, no other witnesses."

Meera started to look around the scene of the crime and immediately noticed the open window.

"Was this always open?" she asked Gokul.

"I don't know. Maybe?"

Meera walked over to the window. "No it wasn't. It couldn't have been open last night. It was raining, the floor under it would have been wet if it was. This has been opened after it stopped raining."

"Maybe the rain dried up?" asked Gokul.

"Possible. I doubt it though. It's getting cold and this window faces west. It hasn't received any direct sunlight yet."

Gokul scrunched up his nose. "Maybe one of the forensic guys opened it to drive out the stench of the body."

Meera ignored him, still looking around. She noticed the photo on the desk and looked at it really closely, specifically at Dheeraj's face, the only one covered in blood. Then, she moved away from the desk and looked at the drops of blood on the floor, dried up. She bent down to look at the blood closely and noticed the toe prints on the blood drops.

"Who are from forensics here?" Meera asked Gokul.

"Jignesh and Kamal, why?"

"Call them here, I don't know them."

Gokul looked down the hallway at the forensic scientists on

the other side of the house. "Jignesh *bhai*! Kamal *bhai*! Ma'am is calling!"

The two fat and old forensic scientists waddled up towards Sunil's room. As they were walking side by side, Jignesh's leg accidentally hit the side of the bucket and Meera cringed. Jignesh apologised to the bucket and the two of them stood in front of Meera, trying not to disturb anything else.

Meera pointed to the bloodstain. "Who's foot is this?"

Jignesh corrected her. "Ma'am that's not foot, that's blood."

Meera sighed.

"There's a footprint here. Have you identified it?"

"No ma'am, we can't," said Kamal.

"Why?"

"Ma'am actually what has happened is that the same blood has been stepped on twice so the prints are all mixing with each other, so we can't identify."

"Sir, I can literally see the footprint right here, what do you mean you can't identify?" questioned Meera.

"We can't identify ma'am," said Kamal, like it was an impossibility.

Before Meera could say anything else, Gokul defused the situation by sending them away. "Jignesh *bhai*, Kamal *bhai*, thank you," he said, motioning them to leave.

The two forensic scientists waddled away. Meera watched them go and then looked at the footprint on the blood again. Then, she stood up and walked over to the bucket and the mop.

"Is that a hammer in there?" she asked Gokul.

"Yes ma'am, we think that's what the victim hit himself with."

Meera bent down to look at the hammer inside the water.

"No way we're getting any prints off that," she told herself quietly. She turned to Gokul. "Any enemies of the victim, someone close to him maybe that would profit from killing him, or maybe someone with a problem with him?" she asked.

"Actually ma'am, I don't think this is murder," Gokul explained to her.

Meera stood up and looked at Gokul with a confused expression on his face.

"You don't?"

"No ma'am. I have a theory." Gokul then proceeded to explain his absurd theory. "Ma'am it's very simple. Last night, our victim, Sunil, was mopping his house, ok? To keep it clean and all, you know? Then, so when he is cleaning and all, mopping and all that, he sees on the floor, hammer. Now Sunil sir is cleaning na. So he needs to clean the floor and all. So he sees hammer on floor and he picks it up, okay? And then, he is looking at this hammer right, when he just, like by accident, just hits his head, like this."

Gokul pretended he was holding an imaginary hammer in his hand and hit himself on his head with it.

"I would know ma'am, all this happens to me all the time. So anyways, Sunil sir *na,* after he hits himself, he drops the hammer, and it falls in his cleaning *wala* bucket. He's moping *na,* remember. To clean his house and all. Now Sunil sir is hurt. So what he does is, he walks, to his table, to sit down and all. Because he is hurt. When you are hurt you want to sit down *na*? So he goes to his table and sits down, ok? So then, because he is hurt and everything, he sees his family photo. Poor man *na,* dying alone? So he sees his family photo. What happens after that? Uhh, oh yes, yes the phone. So the neighbour aunty calls. And he, Sunil sir, he thinks that, yes, I will tell her that I am hurted, and she will call hospital and everything will be ok. So he takes out his phone and he accepts the call, ok? But then, before he can answer only, he is dead. So Menka ma'am also doesn't hear him. Correct *na*? Because he is dead how will she hear him? So after that-"

Meera interrupted him. "Stop." She looked at him in disbelief. "Where do you come up with this stuff?"

Gokul looked dejected.

"Look into the neighbours, ask them if they saw anything, specifically someone running out from this window..." Meera pointed to the open window, "at the time the call was answered."

Gokul pulled out his phone and started typing out what Meera was saying.

"Look into the car they found outside, the i10. Since it doesn't belong to the guy that owns the house, it's probably our suspect's. Make sure those forensic guys do a full sweep, for hair, skin, whatever. I doubt they'll find anything but it's worth looking into. Find out where our victim was last seen, make a proper timeline leading up to his death. Find out about close family and friends, the murderer has to be someone he knew or we would see signs of forced entry and struggle. Specifically look into those people in the picture on his desk and send me their addresses if they're in town. I'll interview them myself. There's a tan line around his ring finger, he's probably divorced."

No ma'am," Gokul interjected. "I have a tan line on my ring finger too, but I'm not even married. My astrologer told me to wear diamond ring on this finger for seven years for good luck."

Meera ignored him. "Find out if he's divorced and look into his ex-wife, maybe she killed-"

"Ma'am," interrupted Gokul again.

"What?"

"Can you not say that?"

"Say what?"

Hesitantly, Gokul answered. "Kill."

"This is a murder investigation, Gokul."

Gokul looked dejected again. Meera once again ignored him.

"I've got some other stuff to attend to, look into this stuff and report to me when you've got something, alright?"

CHAPTER 5: HYBRISTOPHILIA

Meera pulled up outside the small railway station in her police car and walked over to the platform and sat down on a bench, waiting for Inspector Ajay to show up. There were only a few other people at the train station and it was mostly deserted.

Meera stared ahead. There were two lines of railway tracks ahead and beyond that, forests. Meera was distracted by the trees and wondered what was amongst them. An aeroplane loudly flew over the forest. Meera decided to get herself a cup of tea while she waited. She stood up and walked to a tea stall to her right a little further away from the station. She brought back a paper cup of tea but as she was walking back to the bench, it slipped from between her fingers and fell on the floor. She sighed to herself and bent down to pick up the paper cup, just as she heard the train approaching.

Meera put the paper cup into a dustbin nearby as the train pulled over to the platform. Only a handful of people got off, one of whom was Inspector Ajay Rathode, a very young man with a thin moustache. He was in his police uniform when he exited the train.

The wave reached till the tip of Vetal's toes sinking in the sand, before retreating back into the ocean. He was standing facing the Arabian Sea alone at an abandoned side of Juhu beach, looking at the ocean. A sea plane flew over the horizon where the Sun was just setting.

Vetal stood by the ocean for a few more minutes staring at the sea before putting his shoes back on. He was here on a business trip.

Vetal walked a little further away from the ocean towards a couple of rocks on the shore. He reached down and lifted up the giant rock which was just as heavy as it looked, and tossed it aside. Behind it was a locked metal box. Vetal produced a red key from his pocket and unlocked the box.

Inside, in an airtight plastic bag, there was a phone. It was an old keypad phone that looked like it had been in that metal box behind the rock for years. Vetal threw the metal box on the sand and walked away with the phone in his hand.

Only one phone number was stored on the phone, as Pushpak. Vetal dialled the number and raised the phone to his ear as he walked away from the beach towards the crowded road.

As soon as the call went through, Vetal recited the numbers. "12. 1. 3. 300. 60."

The call was put on hold. Vetal waited on the other end of the line. He hailed an autorickshaw and sat inside.

A robotic distorted voice spoke from the other end of the phone. "Status?"

"Survey is complete. I'll proceed with complete annihilation. I need an identity."

The voice on the other end of the line went silent again. The call was once again on hold. Vetal took this opportunity to tell the auto rickshaw driver that he was headed to the Andheri East Railway Station.

The voice on the phone spoke again. "Dr. Venugopal Shah. You will find your documentation by the warplane."

"Thank you," said Vetal. Then, he tossed the phone out of the rickshaw.

Meera was driving in her police car while Ajay sat next to her in the passenger seat.

"... and as of right now I'm staying at Pink Floor Inn, though I'm hoping to find a place to move into soon," he said, talking about settling into the city.

"I've heard the food at the Pink Floor is pretty good," Meera said, making conversation.

"I don't have any meals included."

"Oh."

Ajay and Meera sat in silence.

Meera remembered the Commissioner asking her to be welcoming towards Ajay but she could think of nothing to say to him. She didn't want to talk about work but she could think of nothing else to talk about. So, she finally broke.

"Do you want to hear about some of the cases that we're working on right now?" Meera asked.

Ajay was immediately interested. "I heard about the one with the gang shootout, it seemed really interesting to me. I have a few theories about that actua-"

Meera immediately changed the topic. "Oh no, I was going to tell you about the Sunil case. This guy, murdered in his home, blunt force trauma to the head, no sign of forced entry, blood marks on the floor; and get this: a hammer in a bucket of water, next to a mop. What do you make of that?"

Ajay was put off by the change in topic. "I don't know," he said.

"It's a miracle the forensics didn't find anything, the murder didn't seem premeditated."

"Do you have something in mind? About how it happened?" asked Ajay.

"Not really, it's too early in the investigation," said Meera. Then when another wave of silence settled over the car, she decided to put forward her theory.

"Well, I have a rough idea. I'm thinking, the murderer has to be close to the victim, right? No friends we know of so I'm guessing it's family. Now, we know the hammer belongs to some construction workers who were working near their bathroom a few hours earlier, who said they left it near there. So my theory is that the murderer was invited in by the victim because they were close family, then maybe some sort of argument broke out, the killer found the hammer on the floor and struck the victim on the head. Now, normally a blow like this doesn't instantly kill anyone, it takes at least a few minutes for the blood loss to be significant enough to result in death. Usually, that means that after getting struck, the victim fights back against the attacker. Here however, there is no sign of struggle. So that confirms that the attacker is in-fact some family to the victim that he didn't want to fight against. So he walked over to his desk and looked at the picture of his family before dying. Now, for the mop and bucket, I'm guessing our murderer tried to clean up the crime scene but was interrupted by the neighbour rang the bell. So, he bailed out of the window and left the neighbour to discover the body."

Ajay looks completely unconvinced by Meera's theory. "Huh," he says.

Meera immediately got embarrassed. "I mean, it's not like that's a final assessment or something, it's just a work in progress, really."

Ajay immediately agreed with her. "Yes yes, it's completely normal to have crazy theories at the start of investigations. Hell, I'm sure I've come up with even crazier theories in the beginning of a case. Anyways, this other 'Vetal case', what's the deal with that one?"

"Oh don't worry about that one," said Meera, dismissively.

"He's killed before right?" Ajay asked and Meera nodded. "So he's basically a serial killer. You don't really have a lot of those in India."

"That's not true," corrected Meera. "There's Raman-Raghav, he's pretty popular. Then there's Auto Shankar. Cyanide Malika. Cyanide Mohan. Ripper Jayanandan. There's Stoneman, possibly two stonemen with the same M.O. There were those sisters that killed children..."

Ajay interrupted. "No I mean like, right now."

"That's a good thing right?" Meera asked, suspiciously.

Ajay got defensive. "Yes, yes, of course it is."

"It's a good thing there aren't that many serial killers out there."

"Yes, a very good thing."

"Serial killers kill a lot of people."

"So many people, not good."

"Not good at all."

"Really glad there aren't a lot of serial killers in India," said Ajay.

"Me too."

There was yet another moment of awkward silence.

"I'm just saying..." started Ajay, "I haven't worked a serial killer case before."

"Well I mean, it's not all Bong Joon Ho, Joel Coen and David Fincher."

"Who?"

"I mean, it's not all Anurag Kashyap, Sriram Raghavan and Ram

Gopal Varma. It's just standard police work."

"Yeah I know."

"They're not going to make a movie about us."

"I know I know..."

"It's just police work, Inspector Ajay. Like all the rest of our cases. Let's not overhype something tragic. People have died."

"I understand, I understand."

Another moment of silence.

"Pink Floor Inn," Ajay said suddenly.

"Huh?"

Ajay pointed out of the window.

"Pink Floor Inn. We just crossed it."

Meera starts to take a U-Turn.

That night, a beagle, fondly referred to as Mithai, walked around Meera's small but cosy apartment. The beagle heard his owner outside and rushed to the front door and stood outside waiting patiently. Meera unlocked the door and just as she entered Mithai jumped on her and started to lick her face as she laughed and played along with him.

"How was your day, Mithai?" Meera asked, laughing as Mithai pulled her down on the floor to play with him.

Meera then stood up and Mithai followed behind her as she made her way to the kitchen. "My day was terrible," she told the dog.

She opened a cupboard and took out a large *tupperware* box filled with dog food. She overfilled a dog bowl on the floor in the kitchen with the dog food as Mithai patiently sat and watched hungrily wagging his tail. He was trained well.

"Remember that Vetal case we were making so much progress

on? The Commissioner wants to give it to some inexperienced kid. I met him also today, Ajay. What a bore, I swear. He is looking at the case like you look at Chicken Crunchy Treats."

Meera then opened the fridge and pulled out another t*upperware* box. Inside this, there were cold pizzas folded up. Meera sat down on the kitchen counter with the *tupperware* box and as soon as she did, Mithai rushed to his bowl, but he didn't start eating. Instead, he looked at Meera, listening intently.

"Don't worry though, I'll get Vetal myself, I'm sure of that. There's also this other case I got today, some guy got killed in his home. It looks pretty open and shut actually. I'll talk to the family tomorrow, I honestly think they're only the ones that did it. What do you think?"

Mithai didn't answer, on account of the fact that he didn't speak English.

Meera smiled at him and then reached into the tupperware box to grab a slice of pizza when Mithai barked at her.

"What's the matt- oh, sorry." Meera reached over to the radio on the kitchen counter and switched it on. *Dil Ki Nazar Se* from *Anari* played over the radio. Mithai immediately started hungrily eating the dog food while Meera slowly enjoyed her cold pizza.

CHAPTER 6: ESCHATOLOGY

The Ticket Collector was on the phone with his son when he pushed the door to the carriage open, his hand holding the phone to his ear. He was wearing a white shirt and black jacket with a red tie and a name tag, as was the uniform of a TC. He had a thin moustache over his lip and a laptop bag around his shoulder that he used to keep his writing pad and papers that he needed. The entire carriage was supposed to be empty and there was no one else visible, only the TC talking to his son on the phone.

"How was school?" the TC asked his son on the phone as he looked at the window on the right of the first compartment. The window was left open and outside, it was raining heavily. The howling of the wind was deafening, as were the falling raindrops. Rain gathered on the seat below the window and the TC shut the window with his free arm.

"Did you do that maths project? They will count that for your internal marks, you know?" he asked on the phone.

The TC moved forward, checking left and right to see if any of the windows were open. He had to close them so the seats didn't get wet.

"Alright, fine. I'll help you with that tomorrow, but you have to finish your English homework, you can do that on your own."

The TC continued to move forward, looking left and right to see if any windows were open. The empty train carriage looked eerily unsettling but the TC seemed unfazed by this, given that he had done this many times before.

"Go, finish your homework, brush your teeth and then go straight to bed, alright? Don't watch TV now, it's a school night and it's already late. I'll be home tomorrow morning to wake you up, so sleep well now."

The TC moved closer and closer to the end of the train. On the third-last compartment, he stopped to close a window on the left and then continued forward.

"Goodnight. I love you too." The TC cut the call on the phone and slipped it in his pocket.

He was about to exit and move onto the next carriage, when he noticed that at the very last seat, there was a strange man, sitting by the closed window, with a big suitcase next to him. It was Vetal.

Vetal was wearing a wet green raincoat with the hood covering his head. The wet raincoat was dripping water and the seat all around him was wet. He was wearing his business clothes underneath the raincoat. He had the table open in front of him but he didn't have anything on it. Next to him sat a big suitcase of some sort.

When Vetal turned his head to look at the TC, he pulled the hood down from his head. The TC stared at him for a second. He faintly smelt like rotting carcasses or dead animals, very weakly. Not enough to react but enough to notice. At first, the TC couldn't quite get any words out.

"Sir, you're not supposed to be here," he managed to say.

Vetal didn't react. The TC unzipped his laptop bag and pulled out a writing pad with a list on it and checked it. After double-checking, he put the pad back in his laptop bag.

"The compartment is supposed to be empty," he told Vetal, authoritatively.

"And yet I am here, am I not?" Vetal said, smiling.

The TC moved closer to Vetal. "May I see your ticket please?"

Vetal stared out of the window at the rain.

The TC repeated himself, more firmly this time. "Sir, may I see your ticket please?"

Vetal turned to face him. "You know I don't have a ticket."

Vetal had a very calm voice as he spoke, but there was a definite firmness in his words, and this firmness took the TC aback.

The TC thought about his predicament for a second. There was a set of rules to be followed in a situation like this, as prescribed by the Railways Code.

"Well in that case," the TC started, "... you will have to pay a fine, along with the cost of the distance you have travelled so far. You have to be ejected from the train."

"Tell me officer," Vetal replied, "... do you intend to push me off a moving train?"

"No."

"Are you then going to pull the red chain and delay the train just to leave me in the middle of a forest in the middle of a stormy night?" asked Vetal, inquisitively, like out of curiosity.

"No. You will be ejected at the next railway station after you have paid the fare for the distance you have travelled so far, plus a fine."

"I don't have any money."

"In that case, you will be arrested at the next station." The TC felt satisfied with his own knowledge of Railway Code protocol.

"We could do it that way." Vetal motioned the TC towards the seat opposite him. "Have a seat."

The TC reluctantly sat down opposite Vetal. "The next station will be coming up in the next five minutes or so," he said.

"Worlds have collapsed faster," Vetal said with a smile. The TC replied nothing to this so Vetal continued. "Now, forgive me for being intrusive but I couldn't help but overhear your conversation earlier. Was that your kid?"

The TC nodded.

"Boy?"

The TC nodded again, then answered, "Yes."

"And how old is he?" Vetal asked.

Reluctantly, the TC answered. "He turns ten this October."

"Children are a gift, aren't they?"

The TC couldn't help but faintly smile to himself. "They sure are. Do you have any children?"

Vetal deflected his question. "Where are you from, Mr. Krishnamoorty?"

The TC had a confused look on his face wondering how this man knew his name. Then, he looked down at the name tag he was wearing on his jacket above the chest pocket. The name tag read, 'Gopal Krishnamoorty'.

"Mumbai. You, sir?" he asked.

"You've been in Bombay all your life?" asked Vetal.

"Yes sir, both my son and I. Born and raised."

"How old were you in 1993?"

"Uh... 7-8 maybe? Why?"

"Do you remember the blasts?"

This was a strange question to ask. Still, the TC answered, feeling like he was in some sort of an interrogation. "The Mumbai Blasts? Yes, I do. I was really young but I remember my family watching the news about it. Why?"

"Do you know how far technology has come since then, Mr. Krishnamoorty? Today a bomb about this size ..."

Vetal extended his hands to indicate how big of a bomb he was talking about and it was exactly as much as the suitcase placed next to him.

"... can cause an explosion so big, it could take out cities. We look at the *iPhones* in our hands and look at how far technology has come from those big bulky telephones we used to have earlier but we don't realise that weapons of mass destruction, things like bombs, have evolved at twice the rate our phones have." Vetal paused to let this fact settle in, then continued. "Destruction has always been a step ahead, you know? Right from the very beginning. Today, with the right kind of bomb, anything can be destroyed. These weapons of mass destruction, they don't need radio signals to be detonated anymore. They're so sophisticated, any foreign touch will be enough to set them off."

The TC didn't know what to say. He had a very analytical expression on his face and he was tense, even though he didn't show it.

Vetal changed the topic. "Do you believe in God, Mr. Krishnamoorty?" he asked him.

"I don't know what you mean."

"It's a simple question, isn't it?"

"I'm religious, yes."

"Do you know the story of Kali?"

The TC shook his head slightly.

Vetal narrated the story. "It is said that at the end of times during the *Kali Yug*, Kalki, the last avatar of Vishnu, had to fight Kali, the demon king born from Brahma's back with the sole purpose to destroy. It was the battle of the ages and the entire future of good and evil depended on the outcome. They did have a very legendary battle but at the end when Kali's chariot was destroyed against the rules of combat, he had to flee on his donkey."

The TC found himself getting invested in the story Vetal was narrating. The rain got louder and Vetal had to speak up over the sound of the thundering raindrops, louder.

"He escaped to the citadel of his capital city, *Vishasha*, and locked himself up in his room. It was while examining himself here in the mirror that he realised that he had been mortally stabbed during the battle with the *devas*. The stench of his blood billowed out and filled the atmosphere with a foul odour.

When Dharma and Satya burst into the city, Kali knew this was a battle he could not win. His family of demons and his army had all been destroyed and he had been grievously wounded."

Vetal had a grim look on his face, like he wasn't just telling the story but also reliving it. The TC looked curious.

"Now, some believe that this is where he died. The king of demons, destroyer of the world, dying alone in his room after being stabbed a few times. But I don't think that's true. There is more to the story. In a much older version of the *Kalki Purana*, it states that Kali did not die but instead escaped through time and space, to live in the next *Kali Yug*, in the world today. This version believes that Kali is healing in the evil of this world. That he walks amongst us humans. It says that Kali is still alive today and he could be any one of us. He could be you." Vetal paused for a moment. "Or he could be me."

A flash of lightning illuminated Vetal's face. A few seconds later, faint thunder rumbled outside the train somewhere in the distance. Vetal adjusted his position on the seat and straightened his back.

The TC's leg was shaking restlessly. "That's an interesting story sir, I hadn't heard it before. We should be coming up to the station any minute now," he said.

Vetal ignored him. "What I like about this story is that it lets you decide how it ends. If convincing yourself Kali is dead helps you sleep better at night, so be it. Stories aren't supposed to be true or believable, they're just supposed to be stories, wouldn't you agree?"

The train began to slow down and the TC peeked outside the window to see that the train was nearing the station. He exhaled sharply, heaving a sigh of relief.

"The station is here sir," he said. "I will have to call the station master and the railway police to the train now, I hope you won't cause any sort of trouble. They might take a small fine from you along with the cost of the distance travelled so far, nothing to worry about. If you cannot pay the cost, a hearing will be conducted with the District Magistrate and ..."

Vetal stopped him before he could finish. "No," he said.

The TC felt slightly threatened. After a moment, he said, "Excuse me sir?"

Calmly but very firmly, Vetal answered with a grimness in his voice. "That's not what's going to happen. I am going to stand up right now and walk out of the train. I will be leaving my bag on this seat right here, I advise you not to touch it. You will sit here in your place on your seat and you will close your eyes and you will count down backwards from 30. When you are done counting, you can leave the train and inform the station master that there is a suspicious bag on the seat in the train. You will then walk as far away as you can from the train and find another way to get back home."

The TC started to stutter, out of fear. "Sir, I can't do that."

"Yes you can. I want you to go home tomorrow to your son and I want you to wake him up for school and help him with his maths project. I want you to forget I was ever here. There is no one but you in this train compartment right now, do you understand me?"

The Ticket Collector lowered his voice. "Sir, it's against the policy to..."

Vetal interrupted him, louder. "Listen to me."

The train slowed down even more and the start of the station was visible from the window.

Vetal reached into his raincoat and pulled out a torn one thousand rupee note from inside. It was a third of a thousand rupee note demonetized in 2016 that looked like it was torn recently. It was uneven in shape and was a little smaller than a credit card.

"I'm a fair man," Vetal said. "Since I owe you a ticket, I'll give you a ticket."

Vetal held the torn currency note in front of the TC.

Vetal continued. "This is for when you're in a situation of mortal danger. Say you're stuck in a room, wounded, with the wrath of gods waiting for you outside. What do you do?"

Vetal handed the torn note to the Ticket Collector.

"I want you to give this to your son and tell him to keep it very carefully. It's to keep him safe. You can laminate it later and keep it in the front of his wallet when he's older. Every time you look at your son, I want you to think of how the only reason you are where you are taking care of him is because you chose to do as you are told. Do you understand?"

The TC shuddered. In a voice much lower, almost a whisper, he tried to speak up. "Sir?"

Vetal ignored him. He stood up and began to walk past the TC, leaving the suitcase right there in its place, careful not to touch it. He stood by the door of the carriage and turned to face the TC for the last time.

"We'll meet again Mr. Krishnamoorty, let's hope you don't recognise me then. For now, goodbye."

The train tires screeched. Vetal got off before it halted to a stop.

As soon as he was out of sight, the TC sharply exhaled, like he was completely out of breath. He turned to face the suitcase on the seat opposite him and then looked out of the window to see Vetal slowly walking away from the train in the opposite direction towards the forest in the heavy rain. He looked at the bag again and started to sob uncontrollably. As tears moistened his eyes, he closed them and began to count down. Quivering, he counted. "30. 29. 28. 27."

In the forest, Vetal walked amongst the wet trees, searching in the dark for something.

"20. 19. 18."

In the distance, Vetal spotted what he was looking for. An ancient plane crash site, half buried in the soil, only the wing still a little above ground. It wasn't a commercial plane, but an undiscovered 50s war aircraft that crashed here and went unnoticed since. Vetal walked over towards the wing, and estimating where the cockpit would be, started to dig through the wet mud with his bare hands.

"17. 16. 15. 14. 13. 12. 11."

Just under the dirt, Vetal found a plastic bag inside the cockpit. It was a ziplock bag, recently put there. Inside, there was a wallet, a train ticket and a few other things. Vetal took out the wallet and opened it. Inside, there was an *Aadhar* card that identified Vetal with a picture as Dr. Venugopal Shah. Before the card could get wet, he put it back in the wallet

The TC continued to count down, now sobbing between the

numbers. "10. 9. 8. 7. 6. 5"

Vetal put the wallet back in the plastic bag and put the plastic bag in his raincoat pocket. When Vetal stood back up, a sudden light flashed in front of him. A bolt of lightning struck the exposed wing of the aircraft, right in front of him. So close, he could feel the electricity, like a hard shock from some electrical equipment. Just a few centimetres and it would have been him that was struck.

The wing that was struck by the lightning caught fire. Even in the pouring rain, for just a few seconds, the wing of the war plane was on fire. In the dark forest, the wing of this air plane had suddenly become a source of light, shining brightly upon Vetal.

"4. 3. 2. 1. 0."

The rain put the fire out. Then, thunder rumbled.

CHAPTER 7: ENFRANCHISED GRIEF

The next morning, in the poorly maintained interrogation room of the police station, the TC was sitting with his legs crossed, all by himself. The room itself was designed as a holding cell before it was converted into an interrogation room and so the side facing the rest of the police station was covered with blue tarpaulin, though noise from outside was still audible. Inside the room, there was a table with two chairs on one side and one chair on the other where the TC sat.

Meera entered from under the tarpaulin, pushing the cell door open and taking a seat opposite the TC. It looked as though she was in a hurry.

"Don't worry," she started, as soon as she sat down. "This is not an interrogation, there was just nowhere to quietly talk."

"The TC exhaled, calming himself down. "Good morning ma'am. I am..."

Meera interrupted him. "I'm in a rush actually. Can you skip forward to this man on the train?"

The TC had been waiting in the interrogation room for a while to speak out every detail of what had happened the previous night. He hadn't gone home yet and asked the neighbours to look after his son while he spoke to the police of the town. He was very tired and overwhelmed and really wanted to get everything out, just so he could move on from it and finally go back home.

“Ma’am, he threatened my son and I didn’t know what to do. He was just travelling without a ticket so I didn’t know who he was and then he told me there was a bomb and then...”

“Calm down, Mr. Krishnamoorty,” Meera said, looking at his name tag. He was still wearing the same clothes since yesterday. “Should I bring you some water?”

The TC calmed down a little bit. He had been thinking over what to say to the police for a while so he thought he knew exactly what to say but when he opened his mouth to speak nothing made as much sense as he thought it would. “No.”

Meera ignored him. “I’ll get you some water,” she said. Then, turning towards the tarpaulin, she loudly said to someone outside, “Get a glass of water in here!”

Meera produced an A4 sheet printout of a pencil drawing of Vetal and placed it on the table. “Is that him?” she asked.

The TC took one glance at the drawing and then immediately turned his head away from it.

“It’s him.”

Meera nodded. “Good.”

Meera pulled out her phone and showed the TC a photo of the clothes that were left at the crime scene earlier.

“Was he wearing something like this?” she asked.

“Yes ma’am he was, but he was wearing a green raincoat above that.”

“Alright, good. And you’re saying he talked about ancient mythology and the mumbai bomb blasts?” she asked.

“Yes ma’am, he was telling story about some demon and then he told about some big bomb that can wipe out cities and..."

Meera interrupted him, "What happened after that? Where did he go?"

"In the forest ma'am," said the TC. "He told me to count down and then disappeared into the forest. I counted from 30 and then..."

Meera interrupted again. "You opened his bag, is that correct? What did you find?"

The TC looked embarrassed to answer. "It was one photograph of Mithun," he said, quietly.

Meera sighed. A *havaldar* brought in a glass of water and Meera stood up and took the glass from the tray he was carrying and placed it on the desk in front of the TC.

Meera turned to the havaldar. "Sit down and listen to the rest of what he says, let me know if it's something new. I've got an interview I'm already late for."

The havaldar sat down where Meera was sitting and Meera lifted up the tarpaulin and exited the holding cell / interrogation room.

As she was leaving the police station, she stopped Sub-Inspector Gokul. "Any update on the car?" she asked him.

"Yes ma'am. We booked the car but they're saying there is some sort of chip shortage, so it'll take three months to deliver. It's green colour."

"Not your car, Gokul, the i10 we found outside Sunil's house! Do we know who it belongs to?"

Gokul thought for a moment. "I don't know ma'am," he said.

Meera had never drawn her gun with intent to kill so far in her career but looking at Gokul, she realised that very soon she would. Right now however, she controlled herself. "Find out," she said, firmly, trying her hardest not to scream.

Meera rang the doorbell and waited outside Dheeraj's house. Neela opened the front door. She looked visibly upset about the death of her brother but Meera noticed that she was surprisingly really friendly. Most of the time, the victim's closest family was more often than not visibly distraught at having lost them, even if they weren't close. But Neela seemed strangely at peace with the knowledge of her brother's death.

"We spoke on the phone earlier? I'm Meera." she said, introducing herself.

"Yes yes, sorry. You're with the police right? Come in."

Neela led Meera into the living room and sat her down on the sofa, herself sitting on the chair.
"Ma'am we just have a few routine questions for your husband, won't take much of your time. I am so sorry for your loss."

"Thank you." Then, remembering, Neela asked, "Water? Tea?"

"No, thank you," said Meera. "How are you coping? Dealing with the loss of a sibling can be tough."

"I don't know actually. I don't think it has fully set in yet. I'm keeping myself occupied."

Meera nodded. She noticed the movie *Darr* paused on the TV. Albert Camus' *The Stranger* was lying open, face down on the dining table.

Neela stood up. "Actually, do you mind accompanying me to the kitchen? I'm making tea."

Meera stood up too and the two of them went to the kitchen. "You always drink tea in the afternoon?"

"Yes, green tea. You should really try it," said Neela.

""No thanks. I don't drink green tea," said Meera.

"It's really good for your health, you know?"

Meera considered it. "Alright then, why not? I'll have a cup, thank you so much."

Neela poured one cup of water into the saucepan that already had one cup of water boiling in it.

"So, about your brother. I understand it must be difficult for you to answer questions about him but it will be immensely helpful for us to catch who killed him, any information at all could turn out to be of great help," Meera said.

"Yeah, sure. Whether he has enemies and stuff like that, right?"

"For starters, yes. Did he?"

Neela thought about it for a moment. "I don't really know, honestly. He's not a very likeable man. I feel bad for saying that right now given he's dead and all but it's true. He had a way of being rude to people he didn't have much use for and that annoyed a lot of people but I don't think it would make anyone kill him."

"What about his relationship with his ex-wife?"

"Oh I doubt Sunandana had a problem with him. After the divorce she went off to Thailand. Lives her life like a vacation, teaching preschoolers English. She speaks Thai fluently too. I heard she's a bisexual. The divorce has been good for both of them, I doubt there's any hard feelings there.

The water started to boil again and Neela put the green tea leaves in the water. She took out two mugs. "Honey? Sugar?" she asked Meera.

"No thanks," said Meera.

Neela started putting sugar in one mug. She put seven teaspoons of sugar into the small mug.

"Is it still healthy if you put that much sugar?" asked Meera.

"Oh I seriously doubt it. I just like how sweet it tastes."

"Where was your husband day-before-yesterday?" Meera asked.

"At night?"

"Yeah."

Neela thought about it. "He had gone to meet with some investors that night. He's planning to sell the factory." Then, remembering something, Neela exclaimed, "Oh you know what? I just remembered, he was asking about Sunil that day!"

"He was?" Meera asked, surprised.

"Yes! Oh how could I forget? Right around the time he died too! I asked him, I said, "Why are you suddenly talking about my brother?" and he didn't say anything. I'm sure he had one of those things!"

Meera didn't understand. "Those things?"

Neela started to pour the tea into the mug with a strainer. She first poured it out for herself in the mug with the sugar and then for Meera.

"You know, how when someone dies, you think about them? Those crazy coincidences? My mother-in-law, Dheeraj's mom, she has those all the time. She keeps telling us the story of how the day her husband died, she had this weird craving for Marie biscuit the whole day. Then, at night, her husband, who was working in the factory, had one metal box filled with Marie biscuit fall on his head and he died, god rest his soul, *om shanti*. Nowadays she barely eats Marie biscuit because of that."

"Sounds tragic," said Meera.

Neela handed Meera her cup of green tea and took her cup. Just then, the door to the master bedroom opened and Dheeraj emerged, having just had a bath, wiping his hair with a towel.

He was talking to Neela when he opened the door, the towel covering his eyes. "Neela did you use my shampoo again? It's almost ove..."He noticed Meera.

Neela introduced him to her. "This is Meera, she's the police officer. I told you she was coming *na*."

Immediately, Dheeraj began to breathe faster. He had been preparing for this moment since yesterday. It was only a matter of time before the police knocked on his door and at a time like this it was necessary for him to have his story straight. So, he had prepared for every question that he anticipated coming at him from the police based on the many crime movies and tv shows that he had watched with Neela and came up with a reasonable answer for each of them. Only if he managed to waive off suspicion right now would he be able to get away from this scott-free. Otherwise, he was in big trouble.

"Dheeraj, nice to meet you. How can we be of help?"

"Oh I was just talking to your wife here about how you were asking about your brother-in-law just around the time he passed."

There was already visible stress on Dheeraj's face. "Uh, I don't recall anything like that." He had not anticipated this.

"Of course you do!" said Neela. "You were making dinner and then you just out of nowhere asked about my brother and I said, 'Why are you asking about him?' and you said, 'No reason.' This was just day-before!"

Dheeraj denied it. "I don't recall this."

"Oh come on, how could you forget," asked Neela. "It was less than 2 days ago."

"I mean, maybe I could have said this, I don't recall."

Meera was watching their back-and-forth intently.

"There's no way you don't remember. Maybe you should go for a check-up," said Neela.

"I might have mentioned him in passing, I say a lot of things, it doesn't really mean anything. It's nothing to look into, really."

Meera interjected. "Where were you day-before-yesterday?"

"I was at a meeting," Dheeraj answered instantly.

"What meeting?"

"The meeting. With the Japanese."

"The Japanese?" asked Neela.

"Bankers. Japanese bankers," clarified Dheeraj.

"You didn't tell me they were Japanese," said Neela.

"I didn't want to describe them by their race, Neela. We live in a multi-cultural society, you know?"

"That's true," Meera agreed. "What did you discuss with these Japanese bankers?"

"Just bankers," said Dheeraj. "Forget that they're Japanese. It is irrelevant."

"Oh alright. These bankers, what did you discuss with them?"

"Money. The factory. Things like that."

"What time did you leave?"

"Eight twenty-five."

"What time did you return?"

"Ten ten."

Dheeraj was answering instantly and Meera could tell he had rehearsed these answers beforehand.

"Where did you meet them?"

"At their house. In the restaurant."

"Their house is a restaurant?" asked Meera.

"I went to their house first, then from there to the restaurant," clarified Dheeraj.

"Which restaurant?"

"I don't remember. It was a Japanese restaurant."

"I'm sure it had a name."

"Maybe. I don't remember it so clearly."

Meera looked at Dheeraj suspiciously. "I'm sure you at least remember where it was."

"I can't recall that either," said Dheeraj. He hadn't prepared for this line of questioning.

"What about who these bankers were? Do you remember that?" Meera asked. She could tell he was lying through his teeth.

"They were Japanese. I mean, they had typical Japanese names, how can I remember all that?" he laughed awkwardly. Neither Meera nor Neela found his racially insensitive joke funny.

"So," Meera clarified, "You don't remember the name of the restaurant, you don't remember the names of the people you had dinner with and you don't remember where the restaurant is. Are you even sure that there was such a restaurant?" she asked.

"There was no restaurant. It was a bank," Dheeraj replied.

"Huh?" said Meera.

"Huh?" said Neela.

"I got confused. There was no restaurant."

"Huh?" said Meera, again.

"You know how Japanese work culture is, they don't believe in wasting time and all that. We ate at their bank, discussing business."

Neela interjected before Meera could ask where the bank was. "Wow, you're forgetting a lot of details about last night. I didn't think you would have been drinking, considering you had driven there and all."

"You drove to the bank?" Meera asked Dheeraj.

Neela answered for him. "Yeah, he took the car."

"Well, I'm not going to arrest you for drinking and driving so relax," said Meera, smiling and easing the tension.

"I didn't drink. The bankers, they offered me *sake*, traditional Japanese alcohol, but I refused, on account of me driving."

"That's nice," said Meera. "When was the last time you met Sunil?"

"Who?"

"Your brother-in-law."

"I don't remember," said Dheeraj, without thinking.

Neela suddenly noticed something and her expression changed. She suddenly became very proactive. "We really need to show you to a doctor, Dheeraj. We just met Sunil a few weeks ago when he was here to stay with us because there was still some construction work going on at his new house. He was staying at a hotel at first, Pink Floor Inn, but he got thrown out for screaming at the manager because the breakfast 'tasted like his piss'.

Neela turned to Meera and continued. "We usually didn't meet with him but he had nowhere else to go. He was here for a week, then he left and that was the last time either of us saw him."

Then, Neela awkwardly started to fake-cry. She was no actor and her crying seemed obviously faked but it was incredibly awkward to witness. "The last time any of us would ever see him," she said, between fake-sobs.

Meera was incredibly confused by this interaction and she didn't know what to do. She still had questions to ask and Dheeraj's behaviour was eerily suspicious. Awkwardly, she said, "I'm sorry for your loss."

Still fake-crying, Neela replied, "Yeah you told us." Her voice was a lot less friendly now. "Actually, we're taking the death of Sunil a little harder than we thought we were. It's difficult losing a sibling and all, right? Do you mind coming later?"

"Just a few more questions," said Meera.

"It's getting late," Neela said, now not fake-crying anymore. It was not getting late.

Meera looked around and took the hint. She downed her green tea in one gulp.

"Thank you for the tea, I didn't like it at all but it was nice of you to offer some. I hope to meet you again."

"Yeah, sure, thanks, soon, maybe, welcome, see you soon."

Neela walked Meera to the door as Dheeraj just stood there. He heard the front door slam shut.

Neela walked back over to hold Dheeraj's hand. They waited a few seconds and stood there in silence looking at each other with blank expressions.

Calmly, Neela said to Dheeraj, "You killed my brother, didn't you?"

They both continued to look at each other. Dheeraj's expression changed slowly to guilt.

CHAPTER 8: VOLENTI NON FIT INJURIA

Sub-Inspector Gokul was seated on the sofa in Mrs. Menka's house, asking about what happened at the scene of the crime. Mrs. Menka offers him a glass of orange juice in a tray and he gladly accepts it and thanks her. She sits down on the sofa opposite him.

"Thank you so much for meeting with me," he said. He looked at the notes app on his phone. "Now, since you're the Neighbourhood Safety Head..."

"Head of Neighbourhood Safety now, actually," Mrs. Menka corrected him.

"What?"

"You said Neighbourhood Safety Head but I have been promoted now. I'm Head Of Neighbourhood Safety."

"Oh sorry." Gokul took a sip of his orange juice and realised he didn't like the taste of it. He put the glass on the table. "So, did anyone see..."

"I know what you're going to ask," interrupted Mrs. Menka.

"Really?"

"I know it."

"Oh." Gokul stared at her awkwardly. "Can I ask my question anyway? Just to avoid any miscommunication?"

"No."

"Oh okay. Sorry."

"It's alright. Bottoms up."

Gokul immediately picked up the glass of orange juice and downed it all in one go, even though it tasted terrible. He didn't even know if it was orange juice.

He put the glass down and looked at the next point on the notes app in his phone. "What about close family and friends of the victim?"

"Mr. Sunil had no close friends. Here, I've kept notes of every guest that Sunil has ever officially invited into his home."

Mrs. Menka handed Gokul a handwritten notebook filled with names and addresses and phone numbers. On the page dedicated to Sunil, there was only one name, Nawaz.

"That's it?" asked Gokul.

"That's all he registered for. Before this, there was an elaborate Bhoomi Poojan that Mr. Sunil had organised but he didn't register any of the guests. We tried to shut it down but unfortunately, we were unable to. Since then, only one guest has been registered, Nawaz."

"Who is that?" asked Gokul.

"A drug dealer."

"Huh?"

"He deals drugs. Weed, cocaine, LSD, Doppa, Meth..."

"I know what drugs are. Mr. Sunil did drugs?"

"Oh, lord no. No drugs, recreational or medicinal, are allowed in this neighbourhood without photocopy of prescription from an approved doctor submitted to Head of Neighbourhood Safety. He was a cousin of Sunandana, his ex-wife. Came over to meet with her thinking they were still married. Mr. Sunil wasn't so big on the rules of this neighbourhood. Even this drug dealer, a stupid little idiot man, if I remember correctly, he signed of his own volition. Gave a work address and everything."

"Wow, he really did. That's the gangster Ganpat Bhai's office address."

"People like Mr. Sunil, they think they can take the law in their hands and do what they want. They don't care for society's rules. I think that's why he got what he deserved."

Gokul looked confused. "You think Mr. Sunil deserved to die because he didn't register his guests with the neighbourhood safety head?"

"Head of Neighbourhood Safety dear, say it wrong again and I'll throw you out of my house with a piece of dynamite sticking out of the back of your khaki pants. And yes, that's exactly what I think. There's no justice in this world anymore, no law and order. Believe me inspector, I've been around here for a long time."

"Sub-Inspector, actually," corrected Gokul.

"For good reason. I'll tell you. One night in Mumbai in 1955, I was eighteen years old, walking down the road alone. It was a dark and rainy night and I was drenched, all by myself on the street, as the rain grew stronger. Then, walking towards me from the opposite direction was a stranger."

"What does that have to do with anything?" asked Gokul.

"Do you know who that stranger was?"

"How would I know wh..."

"Have you heard that old S.D. Burman song, *Ek Ladki Bheegi Bhaagi Si*?"

"Yeah, my grandfather listens to it sometimes, why?"

Mrs. Menka smiled. "That stranger was Kishore Kumar. I was the

Ladki, Bheegi Bhaagi Si."

Gokul looked at Mrs. Menka in disbelief.

Meera stood up from her chair in exclamation. "What!?"

She was sitting (now standing) opposite the Police Commissioner in his office. The Commissioner repeated himself nonchalantly. "You're off the Vetal case."

"I heard you! I just don't think you hear yourself. He's spared his first witness and now's when you decide to kick me off the case? What happened?"

"You're doing well on the Sunil murder case, focus on that."

"You of all people know that I can focus on two things at once, what's this really about?"

"I just think it's better for you if-"

Meera interrupted him. "What's this really about, sir?"

The police commissioner sighed.

"Ajay liked the case, so I assigned it to him. He's going over it as we speak. It's his case now."

Meera looked at the Commissioner in disbelief. "He... He liked it?"

"He said he was interested in it."

"You handed him my case, *my case*, because he said he was interested in it?"

The Commissioner stared at her.

"Unbelievable."

"The case needs a new set of eyes on it, Meera, whether you like it or not."

Meera was about to scream at him, but held back. Instead, she walked out of his office and slammed the door behind her.

She turned to the havaldar on the side. "Where's the new Inspector, Ajay?"

"He's sitting in that new cabin by the corner," said the havaldar, pointing down the corridor.

Meera walked over towards Ajay's new cabin and barged in without knocking. He was sitting by his desk looking at something on his computer.

Snarkily, Meera spoke to him. "Hi Ajay, welcome to the police station. You have my case and I'd like it back."

Ajay didn't grasp the situation. "The Vetal case? Yes, yes I do. I actually wanted to talk to you about that."

"No you don't. It's not your case, it's mine."

Ajay was still confused. "Actually, I don't know if you heard, the Commissioner assigned it to me."

"Yeah I heard. I just don't care. I've been working on this case since its inception. It's mine. You want a case, take the Sunil Murder, it's fresh and simple. The brother-in-law did it."

Ajay wasn't looking for trouble. He was still new to town and didn't want to pick fights. "I don't want to get off on the wrong foot here."

"Good, me neither. Hand over my case and we're good, alright?" said Meera. She reached over to a pile of files on Ajay's desk to look for the Vetal case.

Just then, the police commissioner walked in.

"Oh come on Meera," he said, looking at her.

"Sir, we can do this calmly, I just want my case back."

"Oh heck Meera, why don't you understand? Just leave the case alone!"

"It's my case sir!"

The Commissioner had had enough. "Oh it's your case?" the Commissioner said, mockingly. "Then tell me Inspector Meera, what have *you* done for this case so far? He commits headline newsworthy murder, do you get him? No! He kills a witness under our custody right under our very nose and do you get him? No! He kills an entire gang of five people in their house with witnesses that saw him leave and now do you get him? No! He tricks a TC and runs off into the forest and do you get him? No! Be honest, is there even a single lead you're following right now that's going to get us any closer to getting him? Is there? He's been killing people left and right for months now and all we're doing is cleaning up bodies behind him. Last thing we know is he's in some goddarn forest? Heck Meera, we can't work like this. I don't care how much you like this case or how important it is to you or how close you, for some reason, think you are to catching him, you're not getting this case. Are we clear?"

Meera said nothing. Ajay was just standing in the corner listening as the Commissioner scolded her.

"I need an answer, Meera," said the Commissioner.

In a low voice, Meera answered, her head down. "Yes sir."

"Good. Now Ajay," he turned to face Ajay. "This is an important case for our department. Our suspect has left a lot of evidence behind him and the publicity around this serial killer is getting larger. I want to wrap this up fast. If you're not up for the job, say so."

"I won't let you down sir," said Ajay.

"That's the spirit. Are we good?"

"Yes sir," said Ajay.

"Meera?" asked the Commissioner. In her low voice, she answered.

"Yes sir." Then, she walked around the police commissioner out of Ajay's office.

Once her fast footsteps receded, the Commissioner spoke to Ajay. "She's in a bad mood, don't worry about it. She'll come around. She's easily the best detective on our team, it's just that she's getting rebellious. All that power in the badge, sometimes it can get to your head. Happens to the best of us."

Ajay nodded.

The police commissioner too walked out of the room. As he was leaving, he said, "We're getting old."

That night, in the evidence room of the police station, Sunil's phone lit up inside a plastic bag. It was ringing.

The next morning, Sub-Inspector Gokul and Meera were standing by the mobile phone.

"How could you miss this?" Meera asked Gokul.

"I didn't know ma'am. Sorry."

"He's had 16 missed calls!"

"Sorry ma'am."

Meera sighed and unzipped the plastic bag. She pulled out the phone from inside and called back the number on the phone.

Within one ring, someone picked up the call. The voice on the other end of the phone said, "Hello? Am I speaking to Mr. Sunil?"

"No, this is Inspector Meera, may I know who I'm speaking to?"

The voice on the other side of the line didn't answer for a moment, processing this. Then, it spoke up. "Oh. Sir, I'm really sorry I did not want to make this a police issue. I tried to reach out to Mr. Sunil but I missed him leaving the restaurant and then I didn't have his phone number so I got delayed in calling and according to the terms and conditions..."

Meera interrupted the voice. "I'm sorry, what is this in context to?"

"The lemonade of course."

"What lemonade?"

"The lemonade that Mr. Sunil deserved. Isn't that why he's filed a police complaint against the restaurant and got you involved? Because he is justifiably frustrated at not having received his lifetime supply of lemonade?"

"Mr. Sunil is dead," said Meera.

"He isn't suing us for lemonade theft?"

"Mr. Sunil is dead," repeated Meera.

"Oh thank god."

Meera was confused. "May I know where you are calling from?" she asked.

As the afternoon sun shone lightly upon them, Gokul and Meera walked towards Jolly Troll Restaurant from their police car parked a little away as Gokul told her about his interview with Mrs. Menka.

"... and guess what? She was the Ladki, Bheegi Bhaagi Si!" he said.

"What?"

"The girl from the song. That's her!"

"No it isn't. It's about Madhubala. Haven't you watched *Chalti Ka Naam Gaadi*?"

"What?"

"The movie that the song is from. Madhubala's character in it is who the song is based on."

Gokul was dumbstruck. "But she said..."

"Besides, if Mrs. Menka was eighteen years old in 1955, she would be in her eighties today."

Meera pushed open the door to the empty Jolly Troll and entered, Gokul behind her feeling a little betrayed. The waiter was waiting for them by the entrance in the empty restaurant."

"Thank you so much for meeting with us," said Meera to the waiter.

"No problem ma'am. It's the second least I could do."

"Second least?"

"The least I could do was give Mr. Sunil's next of kin the coupon of lifetime supply of lemonade that he rightfully earned," clarified the waiter.

"So, when was Mr. Sunil here?"

"Three nights ago," said the waiter. "He was sitting there," he said, and pointed to the table by the window.

"Was he alone?"

"No ma'am. He was with another man."

"Huh," said Meera. "What did the man look like?" she asked.

"He was funny looking."

"Funny how?"

"Just funny looking. He didn't win any lemonade. Only Mr. Sunil did."

"How long were they here for?" asked Meera.

"They ordered two spicy chicken wings and Mr. Sunil finished both and then they left. I know you might think that that means Mr. Sunil deserves two lemonade coupons but according to the terms and conditions you can only be the bearer of one lemonade coupon at any point of time."

"Did it look like a business meeting of some sort?"

"No, they seemed like they were related."

"Family?" asked Meera.

"Yes, maybe."

Meera pulled out her phone and showed the waiter the photo of the framed photo that was on Sunil's desk when he died. She zoomed into Dheeraj's face in that photo.

"Is that him?" Meera asked.

"There's too much blood," said the waiter.

"So you can't say?"

"Oh no I can. It's him."

"Are you sure?"

"As sure as you can be of receiving a free lemonade coupon when you finish a full plate of spicy chicken wings," said the waiter.

Meera stared at him.

"100% sure," clarified the waiter.

Ajay was sitting at his desk in front of his computer. He had changed his wallpaper three times already, so far. As of right now, it was Saif Ali Khan from *Agent Vinod*. He was incorrectly playing minesweeper when the telephone on his desk rang.

Instantly, Ajay reached for the receiver, but before he picked it up he counted down from five on his other hand to seem like he was busy doing something rather than wasting away his time. Then, he picked up.

"Inspector Ajay here, how may I... excuse me? Yes? Wait, really? When wa... right now? Are you sure? Yes, alright, yes, yes, yes, ok, yes."

Ajay jumped over his desk and ran through the corridor of the police station. Outside, he found sub-inspector Indravadan and he motioned him to follow as he ran past him.

Speaking fast, Ajay said to him, "Vetal. Another victim. Right now!"

Confused, Indravadan followed behind Ajay as he ran outside and got into a police car. Indravadan got in on the passenger seat just as Ajay rolled out and the siren above the white police car started to blare.

However, as soon as Ajay got out on the road, he got stuck in traffic.

"Where is he sir?" asked Indravadan.

"Nearby, I think. Where's Sardar Departmental Store?"

"The one around the block behind the church near the pizza shop?" asked Indravadan helpfully.

"I don't know, I'm new here!" said Ajay, loudly. He knew how important getting Vetal was, he did not want to mess it up.

Ajay honked loudly, even though the siren above his car was blaring. The cars in front of him did not budge.

"Sir there's traffic."

"I can see that!" screamed Ajay.

He looked out of the window and screamed at the person in the car in front of him to move out of the way. The person got out of their window and screamed back. Ajay climbed further out of the window and basically onto the top of the car to look over. The entire narrow road was jam packed with cars.

Ajay jumped out of the window and fell onto the road. "Take over!" he said to Indravadan.

Ajay ran through the traffic of cars and bikes around the block and slipped into a little alley behind the police station. There was no traffic on this street.

Under his breath, he said to himself, "Church. Pizza shop. Departmental Store."

He ran straight ahead. In the distance, he could already see the cross of the church. As he got closer, he heard organs playing. There was a marriage going on inside.

Vetal emerged from inside the church, covered in leaves and a little dried blood. He was walking calmly and putting on the top button of a brand new shirt just as Ajay ran past him without noticing.

Ajay ran straight ahead past the church, behind it. In the distance, he first noticed the pizza shop. Then, near it, he saw the departmental store with the glass door leading inside broken, with a few nearby residents gathered around the store.

Tired from all the running with his hands on his hips, Ajay shouted at the pedestrians. "Police, step aside."

Ajay walked past them into the store. Inside, there was a Sardar on the floor, injured, lying in the glass. Ajay realised that he had been pushed through the glass door into the store. He tried to pick the man up off the floor. He was badly hurt, but nothing permanent.

Ajay walked back out of the store and faced the civilians outside.

"Which one of you called it in?" he asked. One person stepped forward.

"What did you see?" Ajay asked.

"I saw the man arguing with Sardarji, so I called the police. Then, my daughter," he revealed his six year old daughter hiding behind his leg. "... she recognised the man from the drawings. After that, just like that, the big man pushed Sardarji through his own glass door and then-"

Another civilian interrupted him. "They were arguing about opening the shop," she said. "Sardarji said his shop was closed and the big man was saying he wanted a shirt or something and then he started talking about the Gita or something and-"

Ajay was getting restless. He interrupted her. "Did anyone see where he went?"

All the civilians pointed to the back of the church. Ajay ran up to the church and jumped over the wall. On the other side of the wall, before the church on the grass floor, Ajay found a plastic wrapper. It was the packaging for a brand new shirt. Ajay stood up and looked around. Then, he groaned in anger.

CHAPTER 9: PERJURY

Neela's phone rang. She looked at the number on the screen and turned to the other people in the room. "It's the police officer, everyone shut up."

A muffled scream in her background was silenced with a punch. Neela accepted the call. "Hello Meera!" she said cheerfully.

Meera spoke on the other end of the phone. "Hey, are you home right now?"

"No," lied Neela. "We're at the temple."

"Which temple?" asked Meera.

"The Kalki Temple by the old Banyan Tree in Aviao."

"Perfect, that's close to where I am," lied Meera. "I'll meet you there. There's been a development on the case."

"Oh don't bother," said Neela. "We're leaving. We'll reach home in around half an hour, drop by around then."

"Fair enough. See you!" said Meera.

"You too!" said Neela, ending the call.

Then, she turned to the other people in the room and said, "God, she annoys me."

In front of her in the room, there was a hostage tied and gagged to a chair. Nawaz. He was a short and weak looking gangster that came here expecting to sell them drugs. He was wearing a blue-green Hawaiian shirt. There was duct tape on his mouth. Behind him, on the desk, his gun was kept. Dheeraj was standing next to him with a cricket bat in his hand.

"She's coming here in half an hour?" asked Dheeraj.

"Nah. She knows we're not at the temple. She'll be here before that. I'm guessing around ten minutes."

"What do we do?" he asked her.

"We meet her, obviously. Otherwise she'll suspect something is wrong."

Dheeraj pointed to their hostage. "About him!"

"Well it depends," said Neela. She turned to look at him.

Dheeraj started to take off the duct tape from his mouth.

"Do we have to kill you?" asked Neela.

"We're going to kill him?" asked Dheeraj. He stuck the duct tape back over his mouth and Nawaz groaned.

"If he doesn't cooperate, we might have to," said Neela.

"I don't want to kill someone!" argued Dheeraj.

Neela gave him a look.

"Someone else, I mean. We're not murderers, we can't keep killing people!" said Dheeraj.

"You really want to be the one pointing fingers here, Dheeraj? After you killed my brother?" asked Neela. She still hadn't forgiven him for that, but had been much less angry about it than Dheeraj expected her to be, given that he had indeed killed her brother.

Dheeraj got defensive. "Neela, I swear I'm sorry but it was an accident, you have to believe me! He was onto me, there was nothing I could do, he was coming towards me and then I don't know what got into me and I picked up that hammer and..."

"Shut up!" Neela said to him. She had heard his story fifty times over. She turned to the hostage. "Mr. Nawaz, is it? Listen, I'm so sorry about all of this. If it was in my control, there would be no need for all this hostility. Heck, if it were up to me we wouldn't even have called you here. It's just that, you have seen us, we're middle class people and we've got into some trouble recently."

Nawaz's phone started to ring in his breast pocket.

"Oh come on! Really?"

Nawaz shrugged. Neela took the phone out of his pocket and cut the call and put it back.

"Ganpat Bhai called, if you come out of this alive you better give him a call back. Ganpat Bhai, really? That's so Ram Gopal Varma."

Dheeraj pointed to his watch to Neela, indicating to her to hurry it up.

"Right, where was I?" asked Neela, and then answered her own question. "There has been a murder. I need you to make sure someone takes the fall for it. I know you have contacts that do that kind of stuff. We're a poor family but we're willing to pay for it."

Neela looked over to Dheeraj and he reached into his back pocket and pulled out ten pink notes of Rs. 2000 each and one torn piece of paper with Sunil's address written on it.

"That's a lot of money," Neela said, stating the obvious. "Much more than we can afford. We really need this."

Neela took the notes from Dheeraj and counted them out in front of Nawaz. She then put them on Nawaz's lap.

"Keep it. Just get the job done."

Neela held up a piece of paper. "This is the address of where the murder took place. I've written the day and approximate time and cause of death. You just have to make sure someone takes the fall for that murder, alright? Can you do that?"

Nawaz considered it. He looked at Dheeraj and then at Neela. He nodded.

“Fantastic. Now Dheeraj is going to take off the tape and untie you. You better not make any noise and hurry up, okay?”

Nawaz nodded again. Dheeraj took off the duct tape from his mouth and he exhaled loudly.

“Ma’am, why did you tie me up for that? You could have just told me!” he said, exasperated.

“We wanted to be extra sure that you wouldn’t just kill us or something, sorry.”

Dheeraj started untying Nawaz.

“Are you people going to be buying any drugs?” he asked.

“Oh no no, we just said that to bring you here. We don’t actually do drugs,” said Dheeraj.

“You should try ma’am, it’s very nice.”

“I don’t know, what does it feel like?” asked Neela out of curiosity.

“Oh like your body has gone straight to heaven and your mind is in the clouds and you can spin the Earth on your fingers and th...”

Dheeraj interrupted him. “Neela, we’re not buying drugs from him.”

“You’re right, sorry,” said Neela. Neela turned to Nawaz. “Thank you for your help, you’re a lifesaver.”

“Mention-not,” said Nawaz. He looked down at the paper with Sunil’s address on it.

“Wait a second. I know that guy! He’s my brother-in-law!” exclaimed Nawaz.

Dheeraj looked at him confused. “No, he’s my brother-in-law,” said Dheeraj.

"He's both your brother-in-law," clarified Neela. "Dheeraj, Nawaz is Sunandana's cousin."

"I'm related to you?" asked Nawaz.

"Distantly."

Dheeraj looked at Neela with a bewildered look on his face.

"What? I don't know a lot of drug dealers," said Neela defensively.

Dazed, Dheeraj finished untying him. Nawaz stood up from the chair and reached for his gun kept on the table behind him and Dheeraj instantly pulled him back from it.

"You're not getting the gun," said Neela.

"Oh no no, don't worry," said Nawaz. "We are friends now, family actually. I won't do anything with that gun. To be honest, I don't even know how to use it."

"That's not what we're worried about. You see, guns like that cost a lot of money. Think of it as a security. You do our job, we give your gun back to you."

"Oh come on, don't you people trust me?" asked Nawaz, the literal drug dealer.

Both Dheeraj and Neela stared at him.

"Alright, fair," he said, reading the room. "Just put that thing away if a cop is coming and make sure you don't fire it. Those things are loud."

"Don't worry. Thank you."

Dheeraj put the gun inside a drawer amongst socks. Nawaz stood up and Neela walked him out of the house.

Nawaz made his way out of the apartment and then went down the stairs. He took the phone out of his breast pocket as he was going down and called up Ganpat Bhai.

"Hello? Ganpat Bhai? Sorry, I was stuck in the middle of something, long story."

"I don't give a shit," said Ganpat Bhai, on the other end of the line. "Something's come up."

He was a strong man. That's what they all said about Ganpat Bhai, even today after he had turned eighty years old though he didn't look a day over fifty. A strong man. Behind his desk was a life size cardboard cutout of Mithun.

"You know that restaurant I loaned money to? Angelina Jolie-something?" he asked Nawaz.

"Jolly Troll?"

"That's the one. Be there in fifteen minutes. You have a meeting with someone very important."

"What do I have to do?" asked Nawaz.

"Just talk to the guy. He sounds important."

Nawaz was flustered. "Thank you sir for trusting me with this important meeting sir, I won't let you down. I'll get there right away."

"Yeah whatever. If it's a prank caller you make sure to tell him never to call me again or I swear to Mithun *da* I will break his teeth."

"Ok sir."

Nawaz cut the call and brushed past a woman police officer as she was going up the stairs. Then, he took an autorickshaw and eleven minutes later, he was at Jolly Troll restaurant. He paid the driver and pushed the glass door open to make his way inside.

The restaurant was empty, with the exception of the waiter and the chefs in the kitchen. Nawaz looked around and sat down in the first booth he saw. The waiter approached him and handed Nawaz a menu card.

Nawaz looked at the menu card and then handed it back to him. "No thanks, I'm here to meet someone."

"Why don't you order something while you wait?" said the waiter.

"I thought you wait," said Nawaz and laughed at his own wordplay. The waiter didn't get the joke. Seeing that he was the only one laughing, Nawaz also abruptly stopped. He took the menu back from the waiter's hand and looked at it.

"What would you recommend?" he asked.

"Sir, the spicy chicken wings are really popular right now. If you can finish an entire plate of spicy chicken wings then you get a lifetime supply of lemonade, conditions apply."

"What are these conditions?" asked Nawaz, curious.

"Only one lemonade per month, lemonade will only be available in this branch, lemonade will only be allowed to the person holding the coupon, lemonade is subject to availability, lemonade is subject to market risk, lemonade cannot be used to harm or destroy..."

"Ok, then just make it one plate of these spicy wings?" asked Nawaz.

"Anything to drink, sir?"

"No thanks."

"Thank you sir."

The waiter left and went into the kitchen. Nawaz just sat there waiting awkwardly. He stared out of the glass wall at the traffic outside when he saw someone on the other side of the road. It was Vetal, covered in leaves and a little dried blood, wearing the new shirt. He crossed the road without looking at the vehicles coming from either side and they stopped in their way to let him cross over.

Vetal walked over and pushed the door to the restaurant open and sat down opposite Nawaz.

“You work for Ganpat Bhai?” he asked.

“Yes. Who am I speaking with?” asked Nawaz. Something felt off about this man.

“Who I am is the least of your concerns. I need you to make sure a maximum number of the members of your gang are in Ganpat Bhai’s office tonight. Do you have the power to do that?”

“I.. I don’t know. What do you need all of us in one place for?”

“That’s the last of your concerns, Nawaz.”

“How do you know my name?” asked Nawaz.

Vetal ignored him. “Everyone in your gang, in Ganpat Bhai’s office, tonight at 10pm. Can you do that?”

“Sir I don't even know your name, I don't know why I should do this. I need to have a reason to tell people to come to Ganpat Bhai's office *na?* I need to take Ganpat Bhai's permission, I don't even know if he will allow so many people there so late at night. I don’t even know if you’re a prank caller.”

“Do I look like a prank caller?”

Nawaz looked hard at him. Then, he replied, “I don’t know what a prank caller looks like.”

Vetal sighed. “Can you do it?”

“Do what?” asked Nawaz.

“I just told you! Can you assemble all of your gang members in Ganpat Bhai’s office tonight at 10pm?” repeated Vetal. He normally was great at keeping his cool but something about the blank expression on Nawaz's face made him lose it.

“Sir. I don’t think so sir. I’m telling you, no one will listen to me. Why will they listen to me? They don’t even know you. What is your name? They don't know it. Even I don't know it. They don't know what you want to do. And even if they did, why will they listen to me?"

"You want to know who I am?" asked Vetal.

Nawaz nodded. "That might help, yes."

"Alright. Remember that drug operation gone wrong where three people from your gang were killed?" asked Vetal.

Nawaz nodded.

"And recently when those seven members of your gang were killed?"

Nawaz nodded again.

Vetal pointed to himself. "I killed them."

Nawaz looked at him closely. Then he laughed. "Good joke sir."

Vetal rolled his eyes.

"Okay, how about you tell me what you want to do with everyone from the gang in Ganpat Bhai's office? Because I'm telling you, everyone won't even fit inside his office. It's too small. Ganpat Bhai's office used to be big but he had to relocate after the raid. Now it's very small, and nothing good is there and no one really even goes there. Have you taken Ganpat Bhai's permission?"

"No, I haven't, you'll do it for me. What I'm going to do at 10pm in Ganpat Bhai's office today is kill every single last one of you until you're all dead. Do you believe that?"

Nawaz laughed again but seeing Vetal's serious facial expression scared him a little bit. He didn't look like he was joking. Nawaz stopped laughing.

"Listen now," said Nawaz. "I do not appreciate this kind of talk. We're not animals here."

"Yeah we are. We're all animals," Vetal said.

"No we are not. We are people," said Nawaz firmly.

"Yes. We are people. And people are animals. We used to be hunters, kill the meat we eat. Today we might not hunt but we haven't lost a taste for meat. Tell me, doesn't that make us animals? Now, I'm going to ask you once again. Will every single member of your gang be assembled tonight at 10PM in Ganpat Bhai's office?"

Nawaz was unsure. "Asking me many times isn't going to change..."

Just then, the waiter came out of the kitchen door with spicy chicken wings on a tray.

"Wait here," said Vetal to Nawaz, interrupting him.

Vetal walked up to the waiter as he was walking towards their table and shoved the tray off his hands backwards and pushed him into the kitchen through the swinging door. The door shut behind him and through a circle hole in it, Nawaz could barely make out what was happening inside.

Vetal picked up a big knife off the kitchen platform and stabbed the waiter and blood sprayed onto the glass. Then, Nawaz heard as the chefs attempted to fight back against Vetal in vain. It didn't last more than thirty seconds but all that Nawaz could hear from the kitchen were the screams of the chefs as Vetal killed them all one by one. Then, silence. For a minute after that, Nawaz could tell from the sound of the grunting as Vetal picked up the bodies and stacked them on the side.

After that, Vetal walked out of the kitchen, his white shirt covered in blood. He walked over to the tap outside for handwashing, to wash his face.

Nawaz slowly reached behind him for his gun, then realised it was at Dheeraj's house.

As he was washing his face, he said to Nawaz, "I really hope you can make sure all the members of your gang are at Ganpat Bhai's office tonight, Nawaz. Otherwise, I'll be very displeased. And you know what? I'll be willing to forgive you if you're too busy and won't be able to make it yourself. Don't consider it mercy, consider it a reward, alright?"

Vetal saw Nawaz nod in affirmation in the mirror in front of the wash basin where he was washing his hands and face. He closed the tap and turned around and started to undo his bloody shirt.

"I need to hear it from you. Give me your word, Nawaz." said Vetal.

"Ill- I'll do it," stammered Nawaz.

"Do what?"

"Gather the gang in Ganpat Bhai's office tonight at 10pm."

"Good. I need another favour."

Vetal undid his bloodstained shirt and left it on the ground. Then, he reached in front of Nawaz.

"Give me your shirt."

Meera was waiting outside Dheeraj and Neela's house when the door opened and Neela let Meera in. This time, she was a lot less welcoming than before.

"Thank you so much for having me here again. I just had a few more questions so as not to take up too much of your time."

"Well that's perfect because we really don't have too much time to give," said Neela, with a fake smile. She sat Meera down on the sofa and sat down on the sofa next to it. Dheeraj sat down next to Neela farthest from Meera.

"Yeah, we have a movie later," added Dheeraj.

"Oh, which movie?" asked Meera.

"The... that new one. I don't remember what it's called. It's the one with Saif Ali Khan."

"Ayushmann Khurrana," corrected Neela

"Saif Ali Khan and Ayushmann Khurrana," corrected Dheeraj.

"No, just Ayushmann Khurrana. No Saif Ali Khan. There's no Saif Ali Khan movie in theatres," corrected Neela.

"Oh. Right"

"Well it doesn't really matter," said Meera. "I just have a couple of questions, I'll keep it short. There was a vehicle at the crime scene. An i10. It didn't belong to Sunil."

Dheeraj was already visibly sweating.

"We looked into it and guess what? It belongs to you."

Dheeraj froze. He was unable to answer.

"What was your car doing at your brother-in-law's place the night of his murder sir?"

Neela came to the rescue. "Oh thank god you found the car, we were so worried!" said Neela, with not a trace of worry on her face. "It was stolen from us the day my brother died."

"Well, that's strange because you didn't report it missing. Didn't even mention it, actually," said Meera, suspicious.

"My brother is dead, alright? My own brother. You think I have the time? The time to look for some i10? When my own brother, my brother that I grew up with, is dead?"

"Well, you should have mentioned it, it would have been really helpful to the investigation," said Meera, inoffensively.

"It didn't occur to me. We are having a rough time, little things like these slip away sometimes. It's great you found our car though."

"You see, that's something else..." started Meera, turning away from Neela to Dheeraj. "You mentioned driving the car the night your brother died."

Instinctively, Dheeraj replied, "No I didn't."

"Yes you did. Referring to how many details you were forgetting about that night, Neela assumed you had been drinking with the Jap- I mean, bankers, which was surprising to her because you had driven till there. If you had your car to drive to the bank to discuss business and have dinner, how could it have been stolen at the same time?"

Dheeraj's heart was pounding. He felt weak and his hands went numb.

"One more question, Mr. Dheeraj, while we're on the topic of your whereabouts on the night of Sunil's murder." Meera leaned closer to Dheeraj. "What were you doing in the restaurant Jolly Troll with him minutes before he died?"

Dheeraj was about to crack. He knew he was caught. There was no way anyone was talking him out of this one.

His mind wandered off to the gun in his sock drawer. Would he be able to reach it in time? He looked at Meera's holster. She had a gun and was probably trained. He looked around the room trying to evade the question, not moving his head. He noticed a cricket bat lying next to the sofa, within reach. He thought back to how easily he had managed to kill Sunil, even by accident. How delicate the human head was.

Slowly, Dheeraj's hand started to reach for the cricket bat. Right as his fingers wrapped themselves around it, Neela spoke.

"I'm sorry, I don't know what the heck you're talking about," she said, suddenly, with the plainest expression on her face.

Now, Meera was confused.

"Excuse me?"

"Well, for starters, what's this about the car? I don't remember ever mentioning the car to you. Then something about how I mentioned drinking with bankers or whatever. When did that happen?"

Meera exhaled, thrown off. "Th… the last time I was here. Don't you remember? We were talking about how Mr. Dheeraj had gone to the bank to meet with the bankers to…"

Neela interrupted her. "Ma'am, with all due respect, I don't remember any of that happening." She turned to Dheeraj. "Do you?"

Dheeraj dropped the bat on the floor. "N-no. No I don't, I don't remember anything like that."

"I think you're confusing us for someone else, Meera."

Meera was confused for a second. Then it clicked.

With a dumbfounded expression on her face, Meera said, "B- but what about the- the waiter? He saw you meeting with Sunil at the restaurant!"

Neela remained calm and firm. "Well, clearly he's confusing my husband for someone else. My husband has never been to this restaurant." She turned to Dheeraj. "Have you been to this restaurant, Dheeraj?"

"N- no. Never. Haven't even heard of it."

"See. In fact, the night of Sunil's murder, Dheeraj was with me the whole night and we watched *Top Gun* together."

Meera was silent for a second. She was amazed that this was the route they had chosen to go down. She was also convinced now that it was Neela and Dheeraj that had murdered Sunil.

Neela wasn't done. "Now, I don't mean to be rude but your repeated visits are really disrupting our schedule. Don't you have a murderer to catch? Why are you hounding us? We're in grieving, alright? We have a movie to catch."

Meera stood up, very annoyed. "Don't you worry ma'am. Next time I'm here, I'll come with a warrant. I'll make sure you're both locked up for a long time," she said in her anger.

"Oh really? I'll put in a word with your supervisor about your behaviour, your threats. You better watch out now."

Meera was about to retort back but she decided not to. Instead, she said, "I'll see myself out."

Meera made her way to the door and put on her shoes fast and shut it behind her. She had a very annoyed look on her face, like she had been insulted. She made her way down the stairs, ready to order an arrest warrant immediately.

Then, her phone began to ring. It was the Commissioner. She exchanged greetings but it seemed he was not in the mood for them. Something serious had happened.

Halfway through the call, Meera stopped in her steps. She nodded, put the phone in her pocket and then hurried down.

Ten minutes later, she entered Jolly Troll restaurant. Police officers and forensic scientists filled the restaurant. The first time this restaurant had had this many people inside.

Meera walked over to where Vetal had thrown his blood covered shirt. Then, she made her way into the kitchen. Inside, there was blood all over the floor and the equipment, amongst the many rats on the floor scurrying around. In the corner was a mannequin that looked like Mithun wearing a chef's hat. There were blots on the floor where the chefs were killed and from where their bodies were picked up. Meera walked over to the other side of the kitchen, past all the blood. In the corner, the chefs were stacked up, one on top of another. Meera bent down in front of the bodies once to look at them. Then, she turned back to the police officers.

"It's Vetal."

CHAPTER 10: STRUCTURALISM

The police commissioner was sitting at his desk. In front of him were Meera and Ajay.

"So?" he asked.

Ajay started. "Sir, as we speak we have a forensic team goi..."

"I don't care, Ajay," said the Commissioner. He was in a very bad mood.

Ajay looked down. "Sorry sir."

"Vetal has done another massacre. This time it isn't even gangsters, it's chefs. Chefs for god sake! Do you have any idea what the press is going to..."

Meera interrupted him. "Sir, I still think it's not too late for me to get back on the case. After today afternoon's fiasco, I'm even willing to work alongside Ajay to get the Vetal case ove..."

"I almost had him!" interrupted Ajay. He was still annoyed with himself for letting Vetal get away from within his grasps like that. "There was traffic or I would have got him, he was jus..."

"Ajay shut up," said the Commissioner. He turned to Meera. "Please. I already have a headache, don't make it worse. You're not getting the Vetal case, you're lucky we called you to confirm his M.O."

Then, he turned to Ajay. "Forget forensics. They're never going to get anything done. I'm putting the entire force on this. Build a radius, take a sketch around, raise the reward, do everything you can and catch the first person that looks like the sketch and have him arrested before midnight. Tomorrow morning, when the press rolls out a front page article about the five innocent chefs killed in their restaurant kitchen, I want them to specifically mention that the police have already arrested a suspect. Am I clear?"

"Yes sir."

"Get out."

Ajay left.

The Commissioner turned to Meera again. "What is this I'm hearing about harassing civilians? Civilians in mourning, that too. Do you think the media isn't giving us enough grief already?"

"Sir, they're suspects."

"I don't care if they're global terrorists. You can't harass them. Not here. Do you know what the environment out there is like? One think piece on some internet blog can open serious investigations against our branch, do you have any idea what kind of fire you're playing with?"

"Sir I..."

"This is not a matter of debate. I'm not going to debate you, Meera. If you can't conduct interviews without harassing people, hand in your badge and join the paparazzi."

"Sorry sir."

"Better be. How's things coming along on the Sunil death case? Any progress at all?"

"Actually, yes sir. I need an arrest warrant."

The Commissioner exhaled in relief. "Oh finally some good news. For who?"

"Dheeraj and Neela Kumar."

The relief disappeared from his face and he held his forehead in his hand, covering his eyes. "Oh for god sake, did you not hear a word I said?"

"Sir, I know they've killed him. They went back on what they said in my previous interview and completely changed all details of their story. They have money problems which gives them motive and Dheeraj and Sunil were spotted together in a restaurant minutes before he died, something he denied happening."

"We need proof for a warrant, Meera, the court doesn't have time for he said, she said. Do you have a witness statement."

"Yes sir, the..." Meera stops mid sentence and curses herself.

"What?"

"The waiter. The one that died in the restaurant. He was my witness."

The Commissioner seems unfazed by this. "Well he isn't anymore. Do you have any other proof or witness that could help us get a court mandated warrant?"

"Uh- we found Dheeraj's car. At Sunil's place. We think it got there sometime during the murder."

"Your whole case rests on a damn car? Oh come on Meera, do some real police work here!"

"Sir, it's them. I'm sure of it."

The Commissioner blows his lid off. "Oh for god sake Meera. You know what your problem is? Your instinct. You think that just because you have a feeling about something, you latch onto it like it's the only thing there is. Everyone thinks they're the protagonist of their lives, like everything they do has some meaning. But it doesn't. Sometimes we just do things. You can push your understanding of the world onto whoever you want but the truth, the real truth is, the world doesn't care about the logic you throw upon it. We don't make the law, not of the government and not of nature. We just follow the rules and try to understand them, alright? When you're working a case, there's due process to be followed. You're no rebel for disregarding this process, you're an idiot. With an attitude like that, you'll never get anything done."

Then, the commissioner calmed down. "It's been a long week Meera, you've been putting in some hours. We all have. We're getting too old for this. Take some rest."

Meera sighed. The Commissioner wasn't wrong. "Alright sir, Goodnight."

Meera stepped out of the cabin leaving the Commissioner alone. He looked at a picture of Mithun on his desk.

Nawaz was standing outside Ganpat Bhai's office with Sailesh Bhandarkar, another member of Ganpat Bhai's gang. He was wearing a different shirt from last time with a jacket on top of it.

Along with him, a few other gang members were standing around outside while the rest made their way inside to wait. None of them knew what they were there for but somehow Nawaz had convinced them all to assemble inside at 10pm, hinting that there was possible money to be made.

"I've got a job, Sailesh," Nawaz told him.

"Right now?" he asked.

Nawaz took out six pink 2000 rupee notes and handed them to Sailesh. Sailesh didn't take the money.

"12? My rate is 25, you know that."

"They underpaid me."

"That's your personal problem, Nawaz."

Nawaz reached into his pocket and took out another two two

thousand rupee notes.

"You're still short 9," said Sailesh. "Besides, I'm quitting all that."

"You're quitting? You love the job!" protested Nawaz.

"Eh, I used to. Now, not so much. It's just all too different."

"Oh come on man. You are the king of the jail. You're the boss inside, you live like a king, what's the problem?"

"Yeah yeah, all that's fine. I'm just tired of going there, you know? I know all the guys in there, they're just so boring. When you're outside, you get to meet new people. Inside, it's always the same people. Even when it's new people, it's always the same people."

"Oh come on, where's all this coming from?"

Sailesh sighed. He looked around. "You wanna know the truth? I was watching this Jackie Shroff movie, *3 Deewarein*. Changed my life. I don't want to go to jail again.

"Oh come on man, don't let films affect you. You need to do this."

"Nah man, that life's behind me."

Nawaz looked around. "Okay Sailesh, listen to me. I'm helping you here. Something very bad is going to happen and you're my best friend here so I'm saving you. I wish I could save everyone, but I can't. So I'm going to save you. Please take this up."

"What's this about, Nawaz? What's going on?"

Nawaz looked him in the eye. "You trust me right?"

"Not particularly."

"Have I ever let you down before?"

"A few times, yeah."

"Come on, trust me. Please, one job."

Sailesh sighed, but he agreed. "One job. Last one. Then I'm done."

"Fine by me. You need to admit to the murder of Sunil, whom you killed by hitting on the head with a hammer."

"Oh, alright. Come on now, let's go inside, it's almost time," said Sailesh, motioning them to go inside.

"Yeah, yeah. Actually, you have to go confess right now."

"Right now?"

"Yeah, it's urgent."

"Can't I go after the important meeting?"

"No, you have to go right now."

"Right now?"

"Yes."

"At this very moment?"

"Yes."

"That's weird."

"It's urgent."

"Right now?"

"Yes!" said Nawaz. "Yes right now!"

"Ok man, I was just asking." Sailesh took the money from Nawaz.

"You'll thank me later!" said Nawaz, as Sailesh walked away. He said something to retort back but Nawaz didn't hear it.

Nawaz took a moment to look around at all the people around him, making their way inside Ganpat Bhai's office. Then, he randomly ran up and hugged a few people as they were entering. They were very confused but Nawaz didn't care. He had tears in his eyes. Slowly, everyone went inside.

Nawaz stood and stared at the door from outside. Then, he walked away. As he turned to the road, approaching towards him he saw Vetal, coming from the opposite direction. Vetal was still wearing Nawaz's shirt from earlier and was carrying an axe in his hand. Seeing him, Nawaz shivered. Vetal noticed him and smiled a crooked smile at him as he walked past. Nawaz walked forward first and then stopped and turned and looked back to see Vetal turn towards Ganpat Bhai's office and raise his axe to his shoulder. Nawaz turned forward and started walking faster.

After he was a safe distance away, he pulled out his phone to call Neela.

Dheeraj was watching *Drishyam* on the TV when Neela entered from the side, getting off a call. She sat down on the sofa next to Dheeraj.

"It was Nawaz. He said he's made some arrangements to get the job done. He also broke into the crime scene to plant some evidence to really sell it. I think we're in the clear, Dheeraj."

Dheeraj was relieved. "Thank you so much Neela, I really couldn't have done it without you."

"We just have to wait long enough for Sunil's estate to get divided, then we can use the money to get out of the city without having to wait around trying to sell the factory."

"We're leaving the city?"

"Yeah, I thought it would make sense for us to leave all this behind us. Do you not want to move?"

"I do actually," said Dheeraj. "I hadn't thought of it yet but now that you mention it, I do want to move out to somewhere nice."

"With all the money my brother has been hoarding in real estate, we could buy a new house, start a whole new life."

"That sounds beautiful. Where are you thinking?" asked Dheeraj.

"I don't want to make any assumptions and I'm completely fine if you have somewhere else in mind but I was thinking

Chandigarh," she said.

"Chandigarh sounds great!" said Dheeraj. "Great! Wow, you really think ahead with all this stuff."

Neela sat closer to Dheeraj and the two of them shared a silent moment together watching the TV.

Dheeraj spoke. "You know I was really worried you would take it the wrong way?"

"Take what?" asked Neela.

Dheeraj hesitated. "The accident with your brother and all."

"Oh don't get me wrong, I don't support you in what you did. Murder is wrong."

"Yeah, yeah, of course it is. I know that. I didn't kill him on purpose."

Neela nodded. "Well, I promised you I'd be with you through thick and thin so what good am I as a wife if I don't stick by you during the thin?"

Dheeraj smiled and turned to look at Neela. "You really are the best, you know that?"

Neela smiled. They both turned back to the TV to watch the movie.

A violent scene from *Drishyam* played on screen. Neela thought of something. "Actually, I think there's something we still have to do."

Dheeraj looked confused. "Something else? I thought we were sorted. Surely, they won't be able to get us now that we have covered our tracks so well."

"Yeah I know, I know. It's just that..." Neela looked at Dheeraj in the eyes. "We want to be extra sure, right?"

Dheeraj still looked sceptical.

Neela continued. "Just so that none of this stuff bothers us again... in Chandigarh."

Dheeraj looked a little more convinced."

What do we have to do?

CHAPTER 11: THANATOPHOBIA

Late that night, Meera was in her casual clothes, tucked into her bed watching the 1956 movie *C.I.D.* with her dog Mithai, who was also tucked into the bed with her. Mithai wasn't as interested in the movie as she was, and had fallen asleep next to her, his head resting on the pillow.

Like Mithai, Meera too wasn't too engaged with the movie. In the back of her mind, all she could think of was Vetal. Why? If Meera could come up with at least the hint of a motive, maybe she would be able to figure out his next move. It couldn't have been money or drugs. Vetal hadn't stolen anything as yet and he didn't seem like the type to do something like that. Meera thought back to a case she had worked on a few years ago with the Commissioner, the last time a bloodbath like this had taken place. Killing makes people feel like they're in power or in control of their lives. But Vetal didn't seem like he fit into that category either. A large, well built man that can lift up dead corpses in his hands wouldn't feel inadequate or lacking power. There was something else that drove him.

Then there was his M.O. of picking up bodies and stacking them up on top of one another. Clearly, Vetal knew he was morally wrong in killing people. He was religious, probably compensating for his crimes. He frequently spoke about religious things so maybe he felt like a higher power was dictating him to carry out these murders? Meera had read of cases of mentally unstable vigilantes that take it upon themselves to 'cleanse the world'. That would explain why he kills mainly gangsters too. However, Vetal didn't seem like the average mentally unstable murderer. This was not just because he spoke smartly and was completely aware of his actions, it was also because all of it seemed to planned out, too perfectly implemented to be instinctive. Besides, it doesn't explain killing the chefs and the waiter.

Religious guilt was normal amongst criminals, but what about the strange obsession with the Bombay Bomb Blasts? That was more than twenty years ago, why was that such a frequent topic of conversation for him?

There was also the lack of a history. Vetal only appeared on the radar around last month. Yet, he operated like he knew what he was doing. Maybe he had training in the army or some terrorist group but again, he didn't seem trained, he seemed *experienced*.

After Vetal's triple homicide made news, calls came in from other small towns reporting of a similar M.O. There was nothing quite connecting all the cases together and the calls did come from all over the country regarding unopened cases from around five years ago, but up to fifty years ago, so there was no definite timeline that could be drawn with complete certainty. However, Meera deduced that even so, at least some of these cases could be the same Vetal that she was dealing with, otherwise this was way too much of a coincidence. Many of these cases were of similar nature, of small-time criminals and gangsters getting killed in large numbers with bodies often being found at the crime scene being stacked one on top of another.

The more Meera thought about the cases, turning the facts over in her head, the less she had a grasp of the case itself. Why would he leave the TC alive? Earlier Meera thought that this was because Vetal had some sort of a moral code regarding killing innocent civilians but then why would he kill the waiter and the chefs in Jolly Troll. Unless...

Meera felt like she had finally found the right string of yarn to pull at. She got out from under her blanket and muted the movie as she pulled out her phone. Sensing this disturbance, even Mithai woke up and yawned. Then, seeing Meera up to her usual hijinks on her phone, he went back to sleep.

One ring. Two rings. Then, Sub-Inspector Indravadan picked up.

"Good morning ma'am," he said, clearly having woken up from deep sleep. In the background, Meera could faintly hear his wife cursing.

"Indravadan, remember you were telling me about Ganpat Bhai financing a restaurant? Which one was that?"

"Huh? I don't remem- it was Angelina Jolie-something. Why?"

"Jolly Troll?" asked Meera, excitedly. It felt like she had finally figured the case out, at least to an extent.

"Yes ma'am, that. Wh- Is anything wrong?"

Meera didn't answer. She figured it out. Vetal was a hitman of some sort. He got paid to kill off members of Ganpat Bhai's gang. That explained why he killed the chefs too, the restaurant was obviously a front for money laundering and the chefs, well in his mind they probably became a member of the gang by association.

"Is this about the party ma'am? Because we found out about that too late or we would have tried to organise a raid," said Indravadan, over the phone.

"What party?" asked Meera.

"The party. At Ganpat Bhai's office. Is that not what this is about?"

"There's a party at Ganpat Bhai's office? What are they celebrating?" asked Meera, curious.

"I don't know ma'am, one of our informants said there was a party thrown together urgently today afternoon for ten o'clock at Ganpat Bhai's new office. All the members of the gang have to be there compulsorily."

"But what are they even celebrat- oh."

The final puzzle piece fell into place. Meera waved goodbye to Mithai in a hurry and rushed out of her house. This was just a hunch and maybe she was entirely wrong about this but right now, Meera was convinced Vetal was going to cause another massacre.

She rushed into her yellow *Santro* parked on the street and entered the driver's seat. On the messy backseat of her car, she found a plain white shirt and she put it on over her casual clothes as she started the car and drove out.

Through the city, running red lights and speeding through the late night traffic, Meera raced towards Ganpat Bhai's office. The whole ride there, Meera cursed herself for acting so recklessly. After all, there was no proof that something was happening. It was just a hunch. A really strong hunch though. There were just too many odd things happening at once. The last few days, trusting her gut hadn't worked out for her but she couldn't give up on all of that. She might as well give in her badge then. No, Meera had to find out for sure.

Meera reached Ganpat Bhai's office at fifteen minutes past ten. She hurriedly got out of the car and ran up to the office, which was about the size of a large cement barn a little away from the main road. One look at the structure and Meera realised she was right to hurry down here. All hell had broken loose.

Fifteen minutes ago, the unsuspecting members of the gang had walked into the office with no idea what to expect. In the commotions of everyone arguing about why they all so hurriedly had been summoned here, no one noticed that the doors had been locked from the outside with a padlock.

Then, something broke through the window and fell onto the floor. Because of the crowd in the office area, no one immediately noticed what it was. One of the gang members picked it up. It was a grenade.

It was a small explosion, but a loud one.

The window next to it broke. Then, another one. Then another one. Grenades flew in first, went off second, over and over again. The ones that died with the first explosion were lucky. They didn't even realise the horrors of their condition. But a single grenade could only get so many people. The rest had to see what would soon become of them.

When the first window broke, no one paid any attention. Most didn't even notice it. It took the first grenade to go off before the eyes turned. The loudness of it, the smell of burning flesh, the screams of the victims that survived, the strange taste of metal in the air. When the second grenade flew in, everyone was watching.

Of course, the grenade wasn't meant to kill. It couldn't help but get a few victims because of it's very nature but the bombs themselves weren't the attack. Vetal would never spare his victims like that. Instead, they were a warning for the ones that would survive, a hint of what was to come. Vetal was an animal playing with its prey. When the grenades stopped flying through the windows, the door was unlocked from the outside, Vetal standing on the other side of the door, his axe on his shoulder.

When Meera reached Ganpat Bhai's office, none of the members of the gang were alive. One look at the building told her that much, the smoke coming out of the windows was enough indication that the worst had happened. A few pedestrians were standing outside, scared. Some were random passers-by, others were nearby residents. After calling for backup, Meera ran up to them. All of them looked worried or scared.

"Inspector Meera Shrivastav, what's the situation?" she asked them in a hurry.

"There was a loud noise and then screaming coming from inside," said one of the passers-by.

"Someone went inside with an axe!" added a nearby resident.

"Screaming was coming before but then it stopped," added another passer-by.

"Did you see anyone leave?" Meera asked.

"No ma'am," one of them said.

"Leave the area immediately. I have called for backup, everything will be fine."

Meera reached for her gun but realised she was wearing her jeans and had no gun. She rushed back to her car and opened the boot and grabbed a gun from there.

Meera ran past the pedestrians that still didn't move from their place with the gun ready in her hand, towards Ganpat Bhai's office.

She pushed the door forward and entered, ready to shoot. She was stressed but her arms were steady. As soon as the door opened, a little smoke escaped and Meera instinctively held back a cough. The yellow lights were flickering with some of them hanging out from the socket. Some of the furniture was on fire. In the corner, the cardboard cutout of Mithun was on fire but looked eerily undamaged.

On the floor, there were more than a dozen dead and dying people, some not moving, some barely coughing and some trying to scream. She couldn't tell apart those that died in the explosion from those that were hacked up by Vetal.

Meera slowly moved forward through the office, looking from left to right with her gun ready, looking for Vetal. Looking at the bodies, she knew he was right here in this office with her, there was no way he left without stacking all of them up.

Someone loudly coughed and Meera jumped and immediately turned but it was another person on the floor dying. Meera noticed a scraping sound and made her way forward towards it in another room. As Meera moved towards the room, the sound became louder. Then, a grunt came from inside. Meera moved closer to the door slowly so as not to alert the person inside. The lights flickered again. Meera inhaled deeply and then pushed the door open loudly.

"PUT YOUR HANDS IN THE AIR, NOW!"

Inside, there was Vetal with his back to Meera. He had just put down another body and he was just standing there, looking at his stack of human corpses. There were eight bodies stacked already. Vetal was still wearing Nawaz's shirt but it was now covered in blood.

Meera repeated herself. "PUT YOUR HANDS IN THE AIR, NOW!"

Vetal slowly raised his hands up.

"TURN AROUND!"

Slowly, Vetal turned to face Meera.

"GET DOWN ON YOUR KNEES AND PUT YOUR HANDS BEHIND YOUR HEAD!"

Vetal bent down and put his hands slowly behind his head. Meera realised she wasn't carrying any handcuffs.

"Stay right there and don't you dare move or I won't hesitate to shoot," said Meera, loudly.

Vetal smiled. He cleared his throat and spoke in a calm, low voice. "Do you want to know why I killed these people?"

"Rot in hell!" said Meera, immediately.

"Oh I already have."

Vetal coughed and Meera tightened her grip on the gun. She noticed that Vetal had coughed up blood. He looked up to her and smiled, blood coming out of his mouth.

Then, completely unprovoked, Vetal starts speaking, like a priest giving a sermon. "In 1993, there were bomb blasts in Bombay. 257 people died in those blasts. More than 1400 were injured, all in one day."

Meera said nothing. She turned back looking for anybody else to arrive but there was no one. When she turned forward again, she saw Vetal standing up.

"GET BACK ON THE GROUND, NOW!"

"They planted 13 bombs. 12 went off. The 13th didn't. They found it in a scooter some days after the blasts."

"GET DOWN ON THE GROUND RIGHT NOW!" Meera repeated.

"It was because of the one bomb that didn't go off that the entire D-Company went down for the blasts. That was the only piece of evidence that tied the blasts to Yakub Memon. If not for the 13th bomb, the D-Company would have gotten away with bombing Mumbai 12 times."

"ON THE GROUND NOW!"

Meera's finger lay shivering on the trigger of her gun. Vetal looked Meera right in the eye, like he was looking right into her mind. Then, he cracked a smile.

"Or what?"

Vetal took a step towards Meera. Then, immediately he took another step towards her. Meera did nothing.

"That's what I thought," he said. Vetal stood right in his place making eye contact with Meera as she stood there frozen and motionless.

Vetal looked back at the stack of dead bodies on the side. Then, he turned back to Meera.

"Have you read the Gita? Sometimes in funerals, they say this verse. Chapter 2, Verse 27. No one really cares too much for what it means, no one even listens really. It's just something you pay the priest to say when you burn the body."

Meera said nothing. She didn't like being in this room alone with him, especially with all the dead people around them and the flickering lights. She had her finger shivering on the trigger but she knew she couldn't bring herself to shoot. She had pulled out this gun many times before but never shot anyone.

Vetal closed his eyes in prayer and looked up through the ceiling towards the heavens. *"jātasya hi dhruvo mṛityur dhruvaṁ janma mṛitasya cha tasmād aparihārye 'rthe na tvaṁ śhochitum arhasi"*

Then, he opened his eyes and looked at Meera. "You know what that means, Meera?"

She flinched as he said her name. "How do you know my name?" she asked.

Vetal ignored her. "It means that if you are born, you are sure to die. So, it's better not to cry over what is bound to happen. Simple right? Well here's what bugs me about it. When they're reading this at funerals, it's them telling each other not to lament over the dead. They're saying to each other, "hey, it's alright grandma died because she was bound to die." That's not what this shlok means though. It's not to comfort the mourning. It's to threaten the living. Every morning you should recite this shlok to yourself to remind yourself that one day you will meet your end and there is nothing you can do about it. You don't know when or how, but it will happen. It's the end of times, Meera. Do you know how many diseases are out there? Do you know how easy it is to make an RDX bomb and take down an entire city? I'm just a vessel, here to ease your passing. I'm not the devil here, I'm just the priest."

Suddenly, Meera heard a noise from outside and noticed it's the rest of the police force coming for backup.

She called out to them immediately. "HERE!"

Vetal realised this too and smiled one last ugly smile at Meera.

"I look forward to meeting you again, Meera."

Meera flinched at him saying her name again. There was a rustle of multiple footsteps right outside the door and immediately, Vetal fell to the floor on the ground.

Multiple police officers entered the building and Meera pointed them to Vetal lying on the ground and asked them to arrest him. They obliged and put him on a stretcher and handcuffed him to it. Meera was still shivering as they took him away. When he was out of her sight, she finally breathed the smokey air, almost sobbing with fear.

Then, the Police Commissioner emerged from behind Meera and she immediately wiped her face and turned to him.

"So, we got our guy?" he asked her.

"Yeah, the guy they just took away. That's Vetal."

"Him? He looks just as dead as the rest of them."

"He's faking it."

"Oh well, at least we got him. This place is truly a bloodbath, isn't it? Half the force is outside throwing up just smelling this shit. God, you know you've been on the force too long when these things don't affect you as much anymore."

"Yeah," said Meera, looking around at all the dead people around them. "It really is all quite tragic."

CHAPTER 12: VARDØGER

Dheeraj and Neela were still sitting side by side on their sofa, but the mood in the room had changed. They both were looking at the main door, waiting for someone to arrive. The entire floor between the main door and the sofas had been cleared and a large blue tarpaulin had been laid down and spread out. A cricket bat was strategically placed by the doorway.

Dheeraj checked his watch. It was getting late. He was visibly stressed about what he was going to do but Neela was calm, too calm.

"Do you want to go have some dinner after we're done?" she asked him.

"Huh? I don't know, I haven't thought about it. We already ate dinner."

"Yeah, but that was like, two hours ago. By the time we are done, it's going to be late. Plus, we are going to be tired from all the digging. We can go to a late night cafe, eat something light."

"Maybe," said Dheeraj, not really listening.

"I feel like eating lasagna," said Neela. "Like *Garfield*."

"I don't really want to think about eating right now. My stomach is in my throat."

Neela reached over and put her hand on Dheeraj's shoulder.

"Don't worry, it's going to be fi-"

Neela stopped mid-sentence and motioned Dheeraj to listen. Outside, someone was coming up the stairs. The footsteps stopped on their floor and the shadow of a person outside their house was visible from under the door. The doorbell rang.

Dheeraj looked at Neela for guidance, not knowing what to do. Neela motioned him to go and open the door and she herself stood up and went into the room.

Dheeraj stood up from his seat at the sofa and walked over the tarpaulin on the floor to the main door. He opened the door. Nawaz was standing outside.

"Good evening bhaiya, what's this on the floor?" he asked, curiously. Dheeraj looked too nervous to answer. Neela was still inside the room.

Nawaz didn't wait for an answer. Instead, he continued speaking, briefing Dheeraj on the situation. "First of all, your work is done. My guy, Sailesh, he's on his way to the police station as we speak."

Dheeraj was not listening. He kept glancing over at the room, waiting for Neela to emerge.

"Now, for your end of the deal. That gun is pretty expensive, alright? You guys better not have broken it playing around with it. *You talkin' to me* and all that."

"Neela's... getting it," murmured Dheeraj, not really paying attention. What was taking Neela so long?

As if in answer, the drawer shut loudly inside the room and Neela walked out with the gun in her hand, way too casually.

"You really need to keep your drawers arranged better, Dheeraj. I was looking all over for this thing," Neela told him.

"It was with the socks dear, like I said," said Dheeraj.

"Thanks," said Nawaz, looking at the gun. "Now, next time you are in need of drugs or anything, don't hesitate to call me, alright? We're family."

Neela, however, didn't hand the gun to him. Instead, she pointed it at him and asked, "How many people know about what we have done?"

This confused Nawaz. "Excuse me?"

"Don't act smart with me Nawaz, unlike you, I very well know how to use this thing." Neela wasn't lying. She had learnt how to use every major type of gun off the internet years ago and practised regularly.

Nawaz, who had never once acted smart in his life, was very confused. He didn't underestimate what lengths Neela would go to. She had tied him up once, she didn't seem like she would hesitate to do so again.

"I swear, nobody knows. Why would I tell anyone? Even Sailesh doesn't know. In this business, we don't ask questions."

Neela looked at him carefully.

"You have to believe me."

He wasn't lying. She believed him.

She motioned at Dheeraj and on cue, Dheeraj picked up the cricket bat behind Nawaz and hit him right on the head. Nawaz fell to the floor onto the tarpaulin. His brains splattered on the tarpaulin. Blood flew all around them in sprinkles but landed only on the tarpaulin.

Dheeraj saw Nawaz's corpse and burst into tears. Neela immediately took the bat from his hand and threw it on Nawaz and comforted him. She went over and hugged him as he cried. "It's over now. Don't cry. You did well. It's over now, it's fine."

Blood began to leak out of Nawaz's head like a leaky faucet.

Late that night, Vetal was handcuffed to a bed in a hospital gown. Around him were sitting Ajay and the Police Commissioner. Vetal was now wearing thick wiry glasses and had a strangely innocent face.

The Commissioner introduced himself. "I'm Commissioner Abhishek and this is Inspector Ajay, we have a couple of questions about...."

In a cheerful voice, Vetal replied. "Nice to meet you Commissioner. I'd offer to shake your hand but-"

Vetal pulled at the handcuffs strapped to his bed, not allowing him to move. Vetal comically shrugged his shoulders and smiled.

"I am Dr. Venugopalan Shah," Vetal said, introducing himself. "Pleasure to meet you sir, how can I be of help?"

"Doctor?" asked the Commissioner.

"AIIMS Batch of '04," said Vetal, proudly.

Inspector Ajay stepped in with the bad cop routine. "Drop the act, alright? We know you killed all those people in that office and you killed those chefs in that restaurant earlier today and injured that Sardarji this afternoon and before that you killed at least eight, maybe more than that."

Vetal looked at them, very taken aback.

“That sounds awful! Sorry sir, I think you're confusing me with someone else. I just came to the city today in the afternoon. My sister's giving birth. It's a boy, she says. I was on my way to meet her. Took a flight here from Mumbai and all. I have the ticket and everything.”

“Yeah we saw that,” said the Commissioner. Earlier while he was unconscious they had found a flight ticket in his pocket.

“I really didn’t want to get mixed up in all this business, I swear,” said Vetal. “I just want to go and meet my little nephew. My wife and I, we can’t have kids of our own, so it’s always nice when someone in the family gives birth, you know? She couldn’t make it on account of her being a lawyer in Mumbai working a big case right now but I tell you, if she could, she would have made sure to accompany me.”

“And what exactly were you doing in a gangster’s den then, Dr. Shah?” asked Ajay.

“Helping sir, what else? Doctor’s oath. I heard a scream coming from inside and while most people ignore these things I thought it was my responsibility to look into it, on account of me being a doctor and all, and to go check out what all the fuss was about. When I saw all those people injured, I tried to help, but before I could do anything, I’m guessing someone knocked me out cold.”

“Yeah, right,” said Ajay. He put down a sketch of Vetal in front of him. “You’re telling me this isn’t you? Spill the truth pal, or we’re only going to have to make it more difficult.”

Vetal looked at the sketch for a second. “I don’t know sir. It does look an awful lot like me so I do understand why some might think it is,” he said.

“We’ve got an eyewitness coming in now to identify you. After that, it’s all over for you, alright? Might as well confess now and save us all some time,” said Ajay threateningly, trying to break him.

"Sir, I think you're mistaking me for someone else. Like *Don.*"

"You're a don?" asked the Commissioner.

"No no, god forbid. It's like that movie, *Don*. Have you seen it?"

"Shah Rukh Khan?" asked the Commissioner.

"No no, Amitabh Bachchan. I watched it with my father in the theatre when I was younger. In that movie also there's a real Don, who is a bad person, and then there's a normal person, like me, and they both look alike so the police goes after him because they think he's Don and the gangsters go after him because they think he's impersonating Don. I feel like that."

Suddenly, the door was pushed open from the side and the TC entered. He continued to look at Vetal in the hospital bed as he walked towards Ajay and the police commissioner.

"Is this the man you arrested?" asked the TC.

"Yes, yes he is. Thank you for joining us, it's really helpful," said the Commissioner.

The TC didn't say anything. He continued to stare at Vetal in the bed. Vetal stared back at him.

"Is this the man that was on the train with you that night?" asked Ajay.

The TC looked right at Vetal and Vetal looked right back at him.

In his hand, the TC was holding a lamination of the torn piece of the demonetized 500 rupee note that Vetal had given him earlier, tightly in his hand.

"No sir, he is not," said the Ticket Collector, firmly.

"Hold on now, are you sure?" asked Ajay, surprised.

"Yes sir, I am 100% sure. This man is not who was on the train with me two nights ago."

Ajay and the police commissioner looked at each other, confused.

"Alright then," said the commissioner. He motioned the TC to wait outside.

"I'm feel so bad about all those murders sir," said Vetal. "I get scared just thinking about it. So many people in such a small space, lord I couldn't handle something like that. I know being a doctor and all, you get used to the blood but lord, so many wounded people, my heart just reaches out to their families. I wish I could help them all."

"Drop the act, alright?" said Ajay, intimidatingly. "Save the empathy for someone that cares. We know you killed those people and all this is just a well constructed alibi. We have enough eyewitnesses that place you at the scene of the crime," he lied.

The Commissioner joined in. "If you confess right now, we could let you off with just a life sentence. Very few serial killers get that. You could get very lucky, but this offer is only valid if you confess right now. Think about it," he said.

Vetal's expression changed to confusion.

"Excuse me, have I been arrested? I'm so awfully sorry, we have a policy not to talk to police under any circumstance in case we're arrested. God I thought we were just talking here, I could get in trouble for this."

Ajay and the Commissioner looked at each other in confusion.

Vetal continued. "I'm really sorry sir, I'm not allowed to talk to you without a lawyer present. If I could just call up my wife, she's got this big case right now and I wouldn't want to disturb her but I think I'm legally supposed to have her here with me right now."

The Commissioner motioned Ajay to follow him outside.

Neela was driving the car this time. Their *i10* was still impounded by the police and taking it would attract too much attention. So, they had borrowed this *Dzire* from a family friend. This way, in case any evidence was left behind, it could not be traced back to them.

Dheeraj was sitting next to her in the passenger seat. Nawaz's corpse was in the trunk. They had wrapped him up in the tarpaulin and stuffed him in the back. Neela bandaged his head where the blow was to make sure the blood didn't leak out too much, in case it made things inconvenient.

Dheeraj was still a little shell shocked by the whole incident. He had barely spoken since they had killed him. A week ago, Dheeraj had gone his whole life without having killed a single person. Now, he had killed two.

"Is this just who I am now?" he asked Neela.

"What?"

"For the whole of the rest of my life, I am a murderer. Even after we put all this behind us and run away to Chandigarh, I will always remain a murderer, even if nobody knows it," said Dheeraj.

Neela put one hand on his shoulder to comfort him. "You know how in Hindus we have the Atman, right? The soul?"

Dheeraj looked at her and nodded.

Neela continued. "Well in Buddhists, they have the Anatman. The non-self. It's like the opposite of a soul, right? Basically, it means that we are forever changing. There is no permanent self for us. It's like if we had a plane, and everyday we took out one part and replaced it with another. Like the rudder, and the wing, and the seat and so on. So one day we would have replaced every single part in the plane right? It'd be a completely new plane. But then we take the parts that we replaced the old parts with, and we assemble a new plane with those parts. Now which one is our original plane?"

"What?" asked Dheeraj, confused.

"Never mind," said Neela. "It doesn't matter. The point is, nothing is permanent. Especially not people. You're not a murderer, Dheeraj. You're just a guy that was doing his best to protect his family. Now forget about all this."

Dheeraj nodded, but he was still not convinced. "I just feel like-"

Right then, the boot of their car popped open. Immediately, Neela brought the car to a screeching halt on the side of the dark and desolate road by the forest near the highway.

Neela undid her seatbelt and unlocked her door and stumbled out of the car. Dheeraj came out too. Something had clearly gone wrong. Neela looked into the open boot. The bloody tarpaulin was kicked aside into the corner and the floor of the boot had been lifted open. The car jack lay there completely extended.

Immediately, Neela realised that Nawaz hadn't died. One blow with the cricket bat wasn't enough to kill him. He had pushed himself out from under the tarpaulin and using the car jack, managed to break the lock of the boot open and escape. Dheeraj spotted him running, with a hand on his head where the wound was, into the dark forest. The only source of light on the road were the red tail lights of their *Dzire*. Neela and Dheeraj grabbed the shovels they had kept in the boot and followed behind him into the forest. They couldn't let him get away. He was injured, he couldn't get far.

In the moonlight, they could only barely make out what was right in front of them. Neela indicated that they split up but Dheeraj didn't want to. They ran in the general direction where Dheeraj had last seen Nawaz.

Neela split off from Dheeraj, leaving him all alone amongst the trees of the forest. His vision was severely limited and he couldn't even tell which direction he had come from anymore.

He slowly walked through the forest, not knowing where to go. In the distance, he heard a bark. There were wolves in this forest. Dheeraj tripped on the roots of a tree and fell to the ground. He could feel all kinds of insects all over him and he quickly stood up and dusted himself off. He just wanted to go home and get it over with.

Suddenly, from nearby, he heard a loud thud, followed by the unmistakable sound of Neela's groan. Dheeraj turned towards the sound and quietly made his way towards it, the shovel ready in his hand. He realised he was moving back towards the road. Dheeraj could barely make out the figure in the dark, standing with a shovel in it's hand and the sound of heavy breathing.

As Dheeraj moved closer, a car passed by the road and in the yellow headlights, he realised it was Neela and breathed a sigh of relief. Lying on the ground in front of her was Nawaz, this time definitely dead. The car passed by and they were once again in the dark. Neela handed her shovel to Dheeraj and picked up Nawaz's legs. She dragged him away from the direct view of the road. Dheeraj too, threw away the shovels and picked up Nawaz by his hands.

Right then, Neela noticed the headlights of a car on the road slowing down behind them. She turned back to see the headlights of a police car pointed right at Dheeraj and her. Dheeraj noticed too and got worried. Neela too, for the first time, got worried. If the police caught them now, they would actually be red handed. They both instinctively dropped Nawaz's body on the floor and stared at the police car slowly moving, both of them frozen in fear. There was no way the police had not seen them. It was all over for them.

Then, miraculously, the car drove on. It sped forward past them, ahead, ignoring them. Both of them breathed a sigh of relief and hugged each other.

A little later, the commissioner was sitting outside the hospital room that Vetal was in when Ajay came walking towards him from the side. Seeing him, the commissioner stood up.

"So?" he asked.

"I checked out AIIMS batch of '04, Dr. Venugopal Shah is there. To double check, I randomly called two of the students from the batch and sure enough, they remember him."

"So he's not lying about his identity."

"There's more," said Ajay. "The identification in the wallet checks out, so does the plane ticket and also I reached out to the two seats next to him on the flight and they both confirm he was there."

"So we know he was in Mumbai until today?" asked the Commissioner.

"That's what I wanted to find out. So, I called up the hospital he said he worked at and called up the last five patients that visited him. All of them confirm meeting him."

"Did you show them pictures?" asked the Commissioner.

"Yep, sent it to them on WhatsApp. They say it was him."

"And the dates of the other murders?" the Commissioner asked.

"He has a patient as an alibi for every one of them."

"What about the pregnant sister?"

"Her too," said Ajay. "Delivered a boy two hours ago."

"So he wasn't lying about that either."

"No sir."

The Commissioner considered the facts. Then, he asked Ajay, "What do you think of the case?"

"Weighing it out factually, there's enough evidence that this man could not possibly have committed all these murders," said Ajay.

"That's true."

"And the only reason we assume he has in on Meera's word," said Ajay.

"Right," said the Commissioner. "So?"

"I- I don't know. Is anything here enough for a warrant?" asked Ajay.

"Not even a search warrant," said the Commissioner.

"And there isn't even anything to search," said Ajay.

The two of them stared at each other.

Ajay laid out the facts. "There's been two mass murder sprees on the same day. If we don't arrest someone, we're going to get a lot of heat from the press," he said.

"That's true," said the Commissioner. "But think of it this way: We're arresting a well respected doctor that was on the crime scene trying to help. Do you really think that's going to make our position any better?"

"And it's only going to get worse when eventually they realise that he didn't actually kill anyone," pointed out Ajay.

"That'll shut down our entire branch," said the Commissioner.

"Plus, Mrs. Shah has called me three times so far," added Ajay. "I asked around and she's one of the biggest lawyers in Mumbai. We could get into a lot of trouble with this guy."

Ajay and the Commissioner looked at each other. They had to make a tough choice, though really it was just common sense.

"Even putting all the alibis aside, purely on instinct..." started Ajay. "I don't think this man could hurt a fly. I mean, just from the way he talks. He's a sheep."

"I know what you mean," said the Commissioner.

"So, what do we do?" asked Ajay.

The commissioner thought about it for a few seconds. It was really just common sense.

"Ajay, go and unlock that man, make sure this arrest never happened. Tomorrow, I'll make a press statement about how the police department is working round the clock to catch this guy and how we're extremely close and all of that bullshit. I doubt they'll buy it but it gives us some time."

"What about Meera?" asked Ajay. "She's not going to like that we let her suspect go like this."

"This is not Meera's case Ajay, it's yours. I want you to take some responsibility here," said the Commissioner.

"Yes sir, sorry sir," said Ajay.

"Make sure all the police officers stay the night today, we'll be working overtime. We need to show we mean business," the Commissioner ordered.

Ajay went into the hospital to unlock Vetal. The Commissioner sighed. He looked at his phone lock screen of Mithun for a few seconds, before unlocking it and calling up Meera.

Meera was in her car, having changed into her full police uniform. She was driving back to the station when her phone rang. She saw that it was the Commissioner and picked up the call.

"We have an update," he said on the other end of the line.

"Did he confess?" asked Meera, immediately.

"Listen to my voice Meera. Do I sound like I just got a confession?" retorted the Commissioner. He sounded like he was tired, burnt-out and depressed.

"Did he get away?" asked Meera.

"It's not him, Meera," said the Commissioner.

"What?"

"He's not Vetal. This is just some doctor."

"HE'S OBVIOUSLY FAKING..."

The Commissioner interrupted her. "He's got alibis."

"THEY'RE FAKE ALIBI-"

The Commissioner sighed. "They're not fake alibis Meera. I don't want to do this again," he said.

"I spoke to him! I know it's him!" said Meera.

The Commissioner suddenly heard a car drive past Meera. "Are you driving?" he asked her.

"Huh?" Meera noticed two people dragging something suspiciously a little further out from the side of the road amongst the trees.

"Are you driving to the police station right now?"

"Yes?" Meera slowed the car to almost a halt in the middle of the empty highway road and her headlights barely lit up the two people. It was a man and a woman but Meera couldn't tell who they were. She was extremely suspicious of them and planned to get out and check what they were up to so late at night.

"Meera, talking on your phone while driving is a crime, this is what we fine people for. What is wrong with you?" The Commissioner sighed and cut the call, just as Ajay walked out of the hospital with Vetal, now free of the handcuffs. The Commissioner watched as they walked past him and then sighed again.

Meera realised that the commissioner had cut the call and sighed too. She continued to stare at the two people in the distance, who had now dropped what they were dragging and were staring back at her car. She still couldn't make out their faces or what they were dragging but was extremely suspicious of them. Then,

Meera looked back at the declined call on her phone and realised her efforts weren't worth anything. So, she ignored them and drove away. A little ahead, a *Dzire* was parked unattended but Meera didn't think much of that either.

CHAPTER 13: THE MYTH OF SISYPHUS

Meera entered the police station in a hurry. Inside, she was greeted by Sub-Inspector Gokul.

"Is the commissioner in yet?" she asked.

"No ma'am, he's on his way," said Sub-Inspector Gokul. "Ma'am, we have something big on the Sunil case. You were right. It was murder."

"What happened?"

"We got him."

Meera was confused. "Excuse me?"

Sailesh had made himself comfortable in the interrogation room when Gokul and Meera entered. They both stood opposite him on the table while he sat on the chair.

In a monotonous voice he said, "I killed Sunil with a hammer to the head."

"Excuse me?" asked Meera.

"I killed Sunil with a hammer to the head," repeated Sunil.

"That doesn't make any sense!"

"I am deeply ashamed of my actions," said Sailesh.

"No you're not!" protested Meera. "You didn't even kill him, I know you didn't! Did Dheeraj put you up to this? It's Neela isn't it? She put you up to this!"

"I killed Sunil," repeated Sailesh.

"He killed Sunil," said Sub-Inspector Gokul.

"With a hammer," said Sailesh.

"A hammer," emphasised Gokul.

"On the head," Sailesh said.

"Right on the head," emphasised Gokul.

Meera lost it. She put her fist down on the table and pointed her finger right at Sailesh's nose. "Don't you dare lie to me, I know you didn't kill him."

"I killed Sunil. With a hammer on the head. Arrest me please. I confess to this murder," said Sailesh in his monotonous voice.

"Drop the act, alright? Save it for someone that cares. We know you didn't kill Sunil and all this is just a well constructed fall. Where were you the night of Sunil's murder?"

"Killing him with a hammer on the head," said Sailesh.

"No you were not!" protested Meera, angrily. "You were probably at home or something. If you take this confession back right now, we could let you off without a sentence."

"But I killed him," said Sailesh.

"It's a crime to lie to a police officer, you know? You could go to jail for this. Obstruction of justice," said Meera.

"Ma'am, if you do not accept this confession, I'll have to talk to my lawyer."

"That doesn't make any sense!"

Dheeraj and Neela were driving back late that night. They were both tired from all the chasing around and the digging and had finally sat down in peace and were on their way back home. The AC in the car was on full even though it was getting cold out and the sweat on their skin had just begun to dry off.

They hadn't said much to each other. Their problems were dealt with. Within a month, they would move to Chandigarh and leave this all behind them.

Dheeraj turned to look at Neela. When he first killed her brother, Dheeraj thought this was the end of his marriage. He thought she would never forgive him and he would have to spend the rest of his life in misery alone. But somehow, she had stuck by him through his worst of times, helping him out of a situation he didn't deserve to be helped out of. Somehow, this entire situation had brought them even closer together, and now they had their whole lives to live out together.

"Lasagna?" he asked.

She looked at him and smiled.

In the clear night sky above the car, a strange dot of orange light, appearing just like a star, glowed above them.

Meera stood outside the commissioner's office, drinking water to calm herself down. Next to her, Sub-Inspector Gokul stood, reading out loud Sailesh's confession from his phone.

"I would like to admit to the murder of Sunil, whom I killed by hitting him on the head with a hammer. I am deeply ashamed of my action," Gokul read out.

Meera listened with a confused look on her face. "Have we ID'd this Sailesh?" she asked.

"Yes ma'am. He has prior conviction record of murder, he's our guy."

"But how?" wondered Meera. It didn't make sense. He was completely disconnected from the case, had no motive and just appeared out of nowhere.

"Here's how," said Gokul. "Ma'am it's very simple. A few nights ago, our victim, Sunil, was mopping his house, ok? To keep it clean and all, you know? Then, so when he is cleaning and all, mopping and all that, he sees on the floor, hammer. Now Sunil sir is cleaning na. So he needs to clean the floor and all. So he sees hammer on floor and he picks it up, okay? And then, he is looking at this hammer right, when from behind him this Sailesh guy enters. From that window you noticed the other day na? So this Sailesh, he takes the hammer from his hand and just bonks him on the head with it. Like this..."

Gokul pretended he was holding an imaginary hammer in his hand and hit Meera on her head with it.

"So anyway, Sailesh na, after he hit Sunil sir, he drops the hammer, and it falls in his cleaning *wala* bucket. He's moping *na*, remember. To clean his house and all. Now Sunil sir is hurt. So what Sailesh does is, he walks him to his table, to sit down and all. Because he is hurt. When you hurt someone you sit them down *na*? So he, this Sailesh, he goes to his table and sits Sunil down, ok? So then, because he is hurt and everything, he sees his family photo. Poor man *na*, dying alone? So he sees his family photo. What happens after that? Uhh, oh yes, yes the phone. So the neighbour aunty calls. And he, Sailesh, he thinks that, yes, I will tell her that he is hurted, and she will call hospital and everything will be ok. So he takes out his phone and he accepts the call, ok? But then, before he can answer only, Sunil is dead. So he runs off from window only. So then Menka ma'am also doesn't hear him. Correct *na*? Because he is dead how will she hear him? So after that-"

Meera interrupted him. "Stop." She looked at him in disbelief. "Where do you come up with this stuff?"

Gokul looked surprised.

"Ma'am, I have proof!" he protested.

"What? But- This doesn't count!" argued Meera.

"Ma'am it's a confession! I solved the case!" said Gokul.

"It's not this guy, alright?"

"Ma'am but we have hard evidence now! After he came here and confessed, I called up Jignesh Bhai to do another sweep of the house and guess what? We found hair!"

"Hair?" asked Meera, lost. "Whose hair?"

"Sailesh's hair!" said Gokul. "Lots of his hair, actually. It's surprising we missed it the first time."

"Obviously, someone planted it there!" said Meera. "The house has been unguarded for days, anyone could have planted that hair!"

"Ma'am, this Sailesh guy, he has a history of crime. He's already confessed to seven different murders before."

Meera was confused. "If he's killed seven people, how is he still on the streets?" she asked.

"He has strong lawyers," explained Gokul and Meera nodded. That made sense, the justice system was a mess.

"Ma'am we got our suspect, we got our confession. The case is closed. Why do you worry so much?" he asked.

"This guy is not our guy! It's Dheeraj and Neela, they killed him!"

"The victim's family? Why would they kill him? How could they kill their own blood?"

"I don't know! I just know that it's them!" she said. She knew she wasn't making any sense anymore. She felt like she was going insane, like reality was slipping out of her grasp.

Just then, the commissioner entered the police station and Meera noticed him.

"Listen, I don't have time for this right now. Just..."

Meera's words trailed off as the commissioner walked past them.

Then, she followed him into his office behind.

As soon as the door closed, she started. “Sir, did you really let our prime suspect go on the Vetal case?”

“He wasn’t our prime suspect Meera, he was just some guy,” the commissioner said.

“No he wasn’t! He was Vetal!”

“Oh come on Meera, don’t start this again. I’m having a tough time with that case as it is, I don’t want you adding on to all this, alright?”

“I saw him! I saw him stacking the bodies!” she protested.

“He was unconscious the whole time. It’s a miracle he even got away unharmed, with all the toxic smoke and all. He’s just a doctor, Meera.”

“He’s not! He’s obviously lying to you! Why would you believe him?”

“Do you know how many alibis we checked? Listen, I know you feel frustrated that we aren’t able to catch Vetal, all of us are frustrated. But arresting just some doctor is not the way we do things around here.”

“No sir, it’s really him! I don’t know how he has all those fake alibis but he has to be faking them. Maybe he works for some big crime syndicate and carries out hits for them, and it’s this syndicate that gives him this fake identity and alibi.”

“Come on Meera, do you even hear yourself? Crime syndicate? Did he look like Dawood to you?”

Meera was about to argue back but somehow, she had nothing to say. She didn’t even believe herself anymore. It didn’t make sense. It just didn’t make any sense.

Meera sighed and sat down opposite the commissioner. Then, she put her head on the table.

Meera didn't understand the world anymore. It was just bizarre. Her reality wasn't even real. She felt the sudden urge to lie down on the floor. She had been fighting for so long to show people how she saw the world but it just felt like she didn't see anything right. Vetal couldn't possibly be the random doctor that had unknowingly wandered into Ganpat Bhai's office. Dheeraj and Neela couldn't possibly have killed their own blood. They were right, it just didn't make sense. But then, what about what the doctor had spoken to her about when she first entered the office? Or what the waiter had told her in the restaurant about seeing Dheeraj?

Meera's throat was dry and she craved a sip of water. As though hearing her thoughts, the Commissioner poured out a glass of water for Meera and slid it to her side of the table.

Meera picked her head off the table and took a sip of water from the glass.

Then, in a low voice, she spoke. "It doesn't make sense. I've worked off this instinct my whole life and suddenly it's like- it's like I've realised I was fooling myself. It's like I was a terrible piano player but all around me people pretended like I was very good at it until one day I heard my music myself and realised it sounds like shit."

The Commissioner stood up and turned his back to stare out of the window. "Do you remember that case we worked on in 2008?"

Meera looked up at him. "The banker?"

The Commissioner nodded. "Wife, two kids, high paying job, crores in savings, living in a big house in Mumbai, the dream. And what did he do?"

Meera nodded, knowingly.

"I keep thinking about what he said. It was after he was arrested, when we asked him why he did it. Do you remember?"

Meera did remember. "I could do it. So I did."

Meera and the Commissioner shared a look. Then he turned back.

"This job, it really kills you. Not just the crime, all of it. Dealing with people like Vetal everyday, it's all too much. When you're young, you think you're making a difference. That's why I put Ajay on the case. When he looks into the Vetal case, he does it thinking he can make a difference. One less killer on the streets. He thinks he understands people like Vetal, like if he reads enough criminal psychology then he would be able to successfully fix them. But for us it's different. Just the fact that people like this exist in the world, it weighs down on you. Eventually, everyday you start coming into work trying to bury every part of you that makes you human. I mean, just knowing that people like Vetal exist, your whole concept of being human changes. You bury that instinct, try to treat every case like a textbook decision. It's just paperwork. I'm getting too old for all of this Meera. Day after day, over and over again. It feels futile."

Meera nodded but she was unsure where the conversation was leading.

"I'm retiring, Meera," the Commissioner said. "And I'm thinking of recommending your name to this post. That's why Inspector Ajay is here, to take over for you. I want you to be the commissioner. It's a great chair, you sit all day reading case files and telling people what to do. Plus, the pay is good."

Meera was surprised. She wasn't expecting this.

The Commissioner continued. "I think your instinct would be good for the branch. I know you don't feel that way right now but I have faith in you. Your way is different from mine, I think it's better. I've always been very result oriented. Maybe somewhere along the way, I forgot what I joined the force for."

"Sir, I don't want the job," Meera said.

"You don't?"

"Sorry sir, I just don't see myself behind a desk."

The Commissioner looked confused. "Wow. That never occurred to me. Do you really like it out there?"

Meera thought about it. "You know when I started out, I was a sub-inspector in Chethallur, Kerala. Really small village, around five thousand people, but we got tourists. There was this hill, Branthan Mala, on top of which there was the statue of this mad demigod of sorts, Naranathu. My first day on the job, the Inspector told me this story. He said that Naranathu used to roll big stones up to the very top of the hill, which took around an hour and a half to climb, and then roll it back down. Every time the stone rolled down the hill, he used to laugh very loudly at the sight of the rock rolling down the hill. Then he would go back down and find another rock to push up the hill. The last few days, I find myself thinking about him a lot. Why would he laugh at his hard work going down the drain, all of his effort getting wasted? It seems to me, Naranathu never cared in the first place. I think that to him, the rock didn't matter. Why did he push the rock up the hill then? I don't know, and I don't think he did either. It just feels like what we do, it's the same thing. It's a rock pushed up a hill. Now I don't really enjoy pushing the rock even if I'd like to, and I sure wish I could just stop and stare into the sky instead but the truth is, I don't think I can do that. Even when nothing makes sense and my sense of the world is shattered, even when I lose all faith in everything I do, I think I'll still come into work the next day. Just right now, even after everything I did felt so useless, all I could think of was what I would do tomorrow. I don't know how you have the courage to retire sir, but I really don't think I could ever take your place behind the desk."

The Commissioner thought about it. "I don't get it," he said finally, and Meera laughed.

“Yeah, I don’t think I do either. Are you really retiring?”

“Yes, I am,” said the Commissioner. “I want to spend more time with Anita. She’s almost six now. You know what she said to me in the park? She said "*Dadu,* you've got fat." So I told her, I said, "Anita, you shouldn't tell people that, it's rude," and you know what she said? She said, "*Dadu* you're bigger so I can love you more." Can you believe that? She told that to me. My own granddaughter.”

Meera smiled at him. “Goodnight sir,” she said.

Meera stepped out of the police station alone. She stood at the ledge staring outside. There was a cool breeze and she shivered a little in the cold. Meera looked up. The sky was clear and the stars were all visible, as was the full moon, which looked like it floated just a little above the ground. Meera looked at it for a few seconds. Amongst the stars, Meera saw an orange dot that looked a little different from all the other stars amongst it. Meera squinted. It seemed as though the dot was getting bigger with every passing second, like one of the stars was getting closer. Meera wondered if this was an asteroid headed directly towards Earth, all set to wipe off all life in the universe, permanently. It was a grim thought but at a moment like this, it felt almost pleasant.

But it was not an asteroid. As it got closer, Meera realised it was an aircraft. Not just an aircraft but a whole passenger plane, on fire. As soon as she realised this, Meera gasped. It was headed right towards them. Meera looked around but there was nobody else there. She felt she must be the only person in the world witnessing this. As the burning aeroplane flew, it left behind it a trail of thick black smoke. Meera could only watch as she saw it headed right towards her. It was bound to crash.

EPILOGUE

It had been a whole month since the tragedy of the plane crash. Dheeraj and Neela were sitting at a bench, four bags next to them, at the railway station. Though it was early in the morning, the sky was still dark and the railway station was deserted, apart from them. It had gotten colder and both Dheeraj and Neela were wearing heavy woollen clothes.

"Chai?" Dheeraj asked, rubbing his palms together to generate heat.

Neela nodded.

Dheeraj stood up from his seat and walked to a tea stall on the right, a little further away from the station. Neela stared ahead. There were two lines of railway tracks ahead and beyond that, forests. Neela was distracted by the trees and wondered what was amongst them. Very faintly, she heard police sirens in the distance ahead. Then, she saw a man emerge from amongst the trees. She didn't immediately make him out at first but as he moved closer, she realised that he was heavily wounded, running from something or someone. He looked like he had been in the forest for a very long time and his formal attire, white shirt and trousers, were covered in leaves and mud. Behind Neela, a train was set to pass by soon and in the distance she heard the rhythmic clickety-clack sound of the wheels on the rails.

Vetal ran out of the forest from amongst the trees and past the train tracks. Neela watched as he climbed onto the platform. He had a tiny pistol in his hand. Vetal walked past the platform and on seeing that Neela sitting on the bench had noticed him, in an instant fluid motion he shot her right in the forehead. Neela's head immediately fell back and a perfectly round bullet hole appeared between her eyes, with one small stream of blood flowing into her hair as her head lay back motionless on the bench.

Vetal ran past the dead body and he began to make his way past the second set of train tracks behind the bench. Just as the train was arriving, Vetal tripped on the railway tracks and fell on the floor just for a second. He got up immediately but he knew it was too late. He stood up straight and looked to the left just as the fast moving train hit him and killed him instantly.

It was only when the train had passed by that from the forest, Meera and seven other police officers appeared, who had been chasing him so far. They emerged from the trees but stopped at the edge of the second set of railway tracks next to the platform. All of them looked to the right as a train approached, set to stop at the station. It was the Chandigarh Express. It came to a stop at the railway station. It was to wait here for three minutes but no one got off.

Dheeraj walked back onto the railway station with two glasses of tea in his hand, blowing the steam off the glass and taking little sips. He noticed that the train was here and started to walk hurriedly towards the bench. Then, he saw Neela. Dheeraj stopped in his place.

From his hands, the tea fell onto the floor.

---

jātasya hi dhruvo mṛityur dhruvaṁ
janma mṛitasya cha tasmād aparihārye
'rthe na tvaṁ śhochitum arhasi

ACKNOWLEDGEMENT

I'm guessing you have a lot of questions. I won't be answering any of them. Instead, let's talk about the people that made this book possible.

In the 1400s, Johannes Gutenberg invented the printing press.

Six hundred years later, I decided to write a story about a little family meeting going wrong, about two brothers and some chicken wings and a limp and a murder. That story ended up becoming chapter 1 of this story.

Then, I wrote a screenplay for a contest, a short film about a ticket collector that encounters a strange man in an empty train on a stormy night who manages to talk his way out of trouble. I never ended up winning anything but that little story ended up becoming Chapter 6.

There's a couple of people that helped me complete this book. Special thanks to Anuraag Soni, Diya Thakkar, Dumbcoder, Kathan Trivedi, Sagar Megharaj, Nirmal Paul and Vaibhav Shrivastav. All of them read the book at different stages of completion and were in a way instrumental for the next reader's experience, ending with yours. Some of these are friends, family, or just people that I met online, but I like to think they all connected with this story in at least some way or another, the same way I hope you did. Thank you all. You can reach out to me at 1.saahilwritesthings@gmail.com and I will personally reply back to every single one of you because it really does mean quite a lot to me that you have read this far, because so many have not.

Six hundred years ago, it was difficult to get your book printed. Today, it's even tougher.

After finishing this novel, I reached out to thirty publishers.

Ten replied back.

Five sent out an automated mail with 'best wishes', saying they couldn't take the novel for further publishing as it didn't fit their agenda.

Two demanded large sums of money to go ahead with publishing.

One said if I pay a smaller sum of money, I could hypothetically maybe get published.

One said they stopped accepting manuscripts.

One said I had to wait five years.

Zero probably read my manuscript.

Zero read my entire novel.

Zero told me my novel was utter garbage unworthy of ever seeing the light of day.

Zero told me I should quit writing permanently because my writing is too stupid or too absurd or too disgusting or too violent or-

Zero cared.

When JK Rowling talks about how Harry Potter got rejected twelve times because the idea of a magic school for children was too odd, I envy her because I wish someone told that to me. I wish a publisher had read this novel and told me they hated the idea of an idiot killing his limping brother-in-law and getting away with it, or they hated the serial killer with devilish charms and a violent streak, or they hated the poor police woman pushing through a failing justice system just trying to do some good.

Instead, all I got was 'Our Acquisitions Department feels this proposal does not fit our needs at this time. We appreciate the opportunity to consider your work and wish you the very best in your endeavour.'

All I got was 'Thank you for mailing us your submission. However, we regret to inform you that we won't be able to publish your manuscript.'

All I got was ' We're sorry to report that your project is not a good fit for our list at this time. We appreciate the chance to review your submission, and we wish you the very best of luck placing your book with another house.'

All I got was 'At the current time, our unsolicited submissions inbox is closed to submissions.'

Publishing in India is a hellscape. Do you ever look at the rows of books in a large store and wonder what journey they made to get where they are?

They pay for it.

There are agencies, publishing agencies, that ask for large sums of money to represent you. That's the only way this works. You pay them and they talk to the publisher and that's the only way your manuscript ever gets looked at.

If you had a hypothetical greatest book of all time written today in this country and the author of that book cannot afford to pay a large sum to a publishing agency, the chances of it being read are close to zero. There is zero correlation between a well written book and a published book because the way to get a book published simply has nothing to do with how it was written.

If you've ever walked into a book store and got very angry at the fact that every book is obnoxious and cliche, now you know whom to blame. We are no longer a reading public. Books have been reduced only to loathsome self-help guides designed to show off on bookcases and take a picture with on Instagram to pretend to look smarter than you really are.

For six hundred years, the printing press has been the birthplace of the greatest and most important milestones in the human race's evolution. From Charles Darwin's 'On The Origin Of

Species' to Stephen King's 'It', the printing press printed history.

But tomorrow's classics aren't on bookshelves anymore. They aren't in stores and they aren't read in public.

Today, they're on the internet.

www.ingramcontent.com/pod-product-compliance
Lightning Source LLC
LaVergne TN
LVHW041059150826
845673LV00007B/1839
* 9 7 9 8 8 4 4 3 0 6 8 6 0 *